HUNTER AT LARGE

"Dewey's 1961 standalo
Large, is a lesson in how to take one theme
and stick to it. The plot is simple. Nothing
complex. No twists, turns, or surprises.
Nevertheless, Dewey channels his best Mike
Hammer in a man's single-handed thirst for
vengeance."
—Dave Wilde

"Another fine character driven noir from
Dewey, this time telling the story of a cop
solving the mystery of his wife's murder as he
ventures across the county on the trail of the
killers. The emphasis here is on the
exceptionally well drawn characters and their
true and vivid dialogue."
—*GoodReads*

"Fast paced and brutal, without being cheap,
this is a rather unusual story of a young police
detective who constitutes himself avenger and
'hunter at large'. A particularly horrible and
senseless murder of his young wife ... left him
alive and bitter, determined to run down the
criminals and find out the reason for the
crime. How he goes about it—the ingenious
tracking down of the men and the cause—a
case of mistaken identity—makes for
sustained interest."
—*Kirkus Reviews*

HUNTER AT LARGE
by Thomas B. Dewey

Black Gat Books • Eureka California

HUNTER AT LARGE

Published by Black Gat Books
A division of Stark House Press
1315 H Street
Eureka, CA 95501, USA
griffinskye3@sbcglobal.net
www.starkhousepress.com

HUNTER AT LARGE
Originally published by Simon & Schuster, New York, and
copyright © 1961 by Thomas B. Dewey. Reprinted in paperback
by Permabooks/Pocket Books, New York, 1963.

ISBN: 979-8-88601-101-2

Cover design by Jeff Vorzimmer, ¡caliente!design, Austin, Texas
Text design by Mark Shepard, shepgraphics.com

First Stark House Press/Black Gat Edition: September 2024

1

It was nearly dark when he got home. Driving over the narrow dirt lane, rough as a washboard after the dry spring, Mickey Phillips indulged in some private grumbling. It was a hell of a long way home from downtown, especially after an eighteen-to-twenty-four-hour tour of duty. Nobody else on the force lived out in the damn country like this.

He grumbled some more as he left the car parked on the gravel just outside the rundown, barnlike building they called a garage. It wasn't usable as a garage, being still jammed with what Mickey had referred to as junk until Kathy set him straight.

"It's not either junk! It's genuine, restorable antique furniture. You wait and see."

His spirits revived when he started along the side path toward the front door. The warm air was sweet with the fragrance of freshly watered grass and shrubbery and the flowers Kathy had coaxed to maturity out of the dry, long-fallow ground. If it was true that nobody on the force lived out in the country, it was also true that nobody else had a Kathy like his. The "farm" was Kathy's dream and ardent wish, and if Kathy had wanted the moon itself, Mickey would have managed to get himself shot into space with grappling hooks and tow chains.

Luckily, Kathy didn't care for the moon except as a celestial ornament. All she wanted was Mickey, a house in the country and half a dozen kids, in due

time. As he climbed the steps and crossed the worn
boards of the old porch, Mickey had a feeling the time
to start making the kids was any minute now. The
feeling became a certainty when the front door opened
and Kathy personally appeared to greet him.

He noticed the new dress at first sight but said
nothing until the ritual of homecoming had been
accomplished. There was a male prerogative involved.
He had a right to lay hands on his wife any time he
could get away with it, and he nearly always could.
When he finally released her, Kathy was pink,
rumpled, short of breath and delighted.

"Well—! Hello, Mr. Detective Second Grade Mickey
Phillips."

"Hello, woman," he said, closing the door with his
heel, tough-guy fashion. "Come closer."

She held out both hands, backing away.

"Now, Mickey—"

He chased her across the room. She jumped onto
the sofa, vaulted over the back and stood panting with
it between them. He grinned at her lazily and she let
her small tongue protrude pinkly between her white,
even teeth. A rank of pinpoint freckles marched across
her nose, which turned up slightly. She smoothed out
the disarranged waves of her luxuriant blue-black
hair.

"You noticed!" she said. "How sweet!"

He ogled her ruthlessly. She moved out from behind
the sofa warily, removing her apron as she came,
smoothed down the sides of her skirt, hitched up the
bodice, turned archly this way and that.

"Well," she said. "You like?"

"Yeah. I like fine. Only where do you plan to wear it?"

"Just a little something for around the house."

"That's good," he said, "because it fits too good, and I mean everywhere."

"Don't be silly," she said. "There's room for a girdle—if I decide to wear a girdle."

"I know, but how do you get it on and off?"

"If you're a good boy and eat all your spinach, maybe I'll give you a demonstration."

Cautiously she edged out from behind the sofa, while he watched with a mock leer. She made a dash for the kitchen and was almost home free, but Mickey got in one good love-swat as she passed.

"Oops!" she gurgled, and she disappeared beyond the swinging door.

Mickey went back to the bedroom to shed his jacket and gun and heavy walking shoes. Getting into a clean, soft shirt, he gazed at the neat, serviceable, king-size bed and grinned happily.

They dined on pot roast with potato pancakes, sweet-and-sour beets, apple pie à la mode and coffee.

Halfway through the meal, Mickey asked, "Where in hell is the spinach?"

"Figure of speech," Kathy said. "You want to make a complaint, see the manager."

"I can hardly wait to see the manager—all over."

"Patience, Master," she murmured. "We've got the whole night—and all the whole day tomorrow!"

Mickey shook his head.

"Afraid not, honey. I have to report back tomorrow."

The brightness in her face turned to indignation.

"It's your off day! You've been on for twenty hours longer!"

"We're short," he said. "Two guys are—sick."

"Oh no, Mickey!" she wailed, then she broke off, staring at him.

After a moment, she looked away. She knew when he was not exactly lying but glossing over the harsh realities of his profession. The truth was that the two guys were more than sick. One, Sergeant Duffy, was dead; and the second, a detective named Russo, was in critical condition in County Hospital, suffering from deep knife wounds in the neck and abdomen—the result of a savage, unexpected encounter in a warehouse near the railroad yards.

Mickey was lucky (from one, personal point of view) to be home at all. He had volunteered for continuing duty, along with everyone else in the house at the time. But he hadn't been chosen. Captain Andrews had made his selection from among the most experienced men on the force and those who had been on a short tour. The rest he had ordered to follow their regular schedules, except that in Mickey's case, the usual twenty-four hours off would be cut to twelve.

"We've got other business around here, too," Captain Andrews had said, "so the rest of you had better get your sleep."

So, he was home on orders, not by choice; but now, being home, he had made up his mind to enjoy it. Kathy pouted for a while but worked out of it all right by the time they finished the pie and ice cream.

"After all," Mickey said, "you were half right. We've got the whole night."

"Then let's make the best of it," Kathy said, getting up and bustling about the table. "I'll get the dishes done right away."

"I'll help."

"No, honey." She pushed him toward the big leather chair beside the radio. "You sit down and relax. The Cubs are in St. Louis tonight."

"All right, I'll sit down, but between you and the Cubs, I won't do much relaxing."

She kissed him quickly and turned back to the table.

"I didn't mean you should relax altogether," she said.

He settled back as she carried an armload of dishes to the kitchen. He turned on the radio and monkeyed with the dial till he found the game in St. Louis. It turned out to be a slow pitchers' duel and he only half listened. Preoccupied with what had happened to Sergeant Duffy and poor Russo, he brooded savagely. He could not have told her the score, in the third inning, when Kathy came in from the kitchen, rubbing lotion into her hands.

She stopped short at the sight of his clenched fists on the chair arms and the way his toes were turned in and raised off the floor, and the look on his face, twisted and full of fury.

He cleared his mind by sheer force, made his hands loosen, planted his feet firmly and smiled. But he didn't fool Kathy. She settled herself on his lap and kissed his eyes and mouth.

"You'll get your chance, darling," she said.

"Sure."

She placed the tip of her finger against his nose and tapped with it to make her points.

"I know you will," she said, "because in the first place, you are not an ordinary cop; you are Mickey Phillips. In the second place, you are the smartest cop in the world."

Her finger slid up along the bridge of his nose. She traced the curving line of his full black brows, first one, then the other. Her hand went up and her fingers lingered over his thick, close-cropped black hair.

"You're smart enough," she said, "to do it the right way, so you won't get hurt, huh? You have a nice dreamy face and I don't want to see it messed up."

"I'll wear some kind of football headgear. How about that?"

"I don't care how you do it, honey, but take care of yourself. So you can take care of me. And the kids."

She was rubbing her nose against his.

"What kids?" he mumbled.

"You know what kids."

Her mouth found his and her tongue slid slyly, flirtatiously between his teeth. He nipped at it lightly. Kathy wriggled.

"Hey," she said softly.

"Yeah. About those kids."

"Do you think I'll make a good mother?"

"How can I tell without a little inspection?"

"Oh, already you're an inspector!"

"You know it. How about that demonstration?"

"What demonstration?"

He tightened his arms around her waist. Kathy gasped.

"Ooh, muscles!"

"I got all kinds of muscles. Come on, make with the show."

"Squeeze me again."

He did it. She started kicking and he released her and she got off his lap.

"You'll have to come in the boodwah," she said, walking away, her hands plucking at the sides of her skirt. "I'm not going to do a strip tease in the living room with the shades up."

He got up and went after her and there was no more hate in his face. He was halfway across the room when Kathy disappeared in the dark bedroom hall. He changed direction suddenly, went to the door and made sure the night latch was thrown. Unexpected visitors were few and far between out here but they did have this one nosy neighbor, Mrs. Crale, who lived with a bunch of cats about a quarter mile down the road and sometimes got lonely for human companionship.

When he got to the open bedroom door, the light was on and Kathy was standing in the middle of the room with her back to him, her fingers teasing at the dress. He caught her eye, and most of the rest of her, in the mirror above the bureau and smiled. It was supposed to be a wolfish smile.

But what Mickey Phillips was really thinking was, How did it happen to me? A girl like her, out of all the guys she could have had, how come me?

They had been married for nearly two years and he still had this feeling of amazement on the average of three times a day.

She looked at him over her shoulder and he could

tell she was excited by the rising pink in her face.

Kathy, he thought. So sweet, so hot, so good—my Kathy.

"You see, about this dress," she chattered, "it's simple. There's a zipper, for instance, right here."

Her fingers fumbled a little beside her right breast, found the zipper and pulled it down to her waist. She ran her tongue over her lips and looked at him coyly.

"Very clever," he said. "So then?"

"So what?"

"So what do you do next? Slip out through the slit in the side?"

"No, silly. You have to pick it up by the hem and pull it off. Over the head like."

"So go ahead."

She pursed her lips at him and her eyes went wide. "Oh sir! Must I?"

He took a step into the room.

"You wouldn't want that nice new dress to get mussed up, would you?" he said.

"Okay, okay," she said hastily. "Here goes."

She gathered it up below and began slowly to raise it with both hands. Halfway up the backs of her firm, round thighs, it halted.

"Made it myself, you know," she said. "Not counting the labor, it cost three dollars and thirty-eight cents."

"Beautiful Kathy," he said.

She sighed.

"I don't know," she said. "A girl can work her fingers to the bone, right to the bone!"

"I'm bleeding," he said.

She twisted her body, trying to look down at her

naked legs.

"Are my seams straight?" she said.

"I can't tell yet."

She lifted the dress a little higher.

"Got to go a lot higher than that, baby," he said. "At least a couple of feet."

"Oh you brute. You big, masterful hunk of muscle."

She raised the hem, up and up, and he watched with rising, thudding excitement as she unveiled the lovely, firm, sparsely freckled flesh, the swelling roundnesses above her thighs, the straight back, small at the waist then broadening, wedgelike, to her rounding, feminine shoulders. She bent slightly and pulled the dress off over her head, then straightened and stood quietly, her eyes fallen, holding the dress in one hand at her side. His throat ached at the perfection of her always new, always breath-taking loveliness.

My Kathy, he thought again; out of all those other guys she could have picked …

He touched her shoulders with tenderness. She was shy for a moment and hid her face on his chest. He drew her toward the bed, sat down on the edge and held her lightly at the hips, kissed the tips of her high, taut breasts. She shivered and ran her hand over his hair.

"Ah, Kathy—" he said.

"You were saying?" she said. "About kids? Babies, like?"

"Uh-huh. Which will it be? Boy or girl?"

"A boy first, I think. Can you do that?"

"Easy as flipping a coin."

"Yeah," she said on her breath. "And more fun."

"Much more fun."

Standing before him, she started to unbutton his shirt. He filled his arms with the warm fullness of her thighs and buttocks and nuzzled her midriff roughly. There was a knock at the door.

Kathy's hand tightened in his hair.

"Wait!" she whispered. "Maybe they'll go away."

He waited, hugging her. The knock came again, louder. Mickey groaned.

"Probably Old Lady Crale," he said. "I'll get rid of her, tell her you're sick."

Kathy caught his arm.

"No, don't tell her that. She'll be back in fifteen minutes with a bowl of hot soup."

"I'll think of something. Don't go away."

The knock sounded once more, insistent, when he got to the hall.

"I'm coming," he growled. "Keep your shirtwaist on."

He crossed the room quickly, grasped and twisted the door knob and opened wide. The hair at the back of his scalp bristled. Two men stood outside at the threshold: one tall, well built, wearing a gray felt hat; the other stocky, older, in thick glasses, with a bonnet of some kind on his head—a French beret.

"Mickey Phillips live here?" the tall one said.

"What about it?" Mickey said.

The stocky one pulled a white card from his breast pocket and held it out. As Mickey's eyes dropped to it, the tall one took one step inside and slammed his fist into Mickey's belly. He doubled downward in sudden agony but held on long enough to swing once at the other's head. But he was off balance, the blow glanced off a hard cheekbone and the tall one hit him again in the belly.

Mickey sagged. He saw the hand go up and the sap start down, and he tried to dodge, but it struck him on the neck, choking off his wind. It rose and fell twice more, landing once on the top of his head and once behind his right ear. He tried to yell something at Kathy, but afterward he never was sure whether he had made any sound. He collapsed at the tall one's feet and by the time he hit the floor he was unconscious.

He woke to a nightmare of horror beside which all the atrocities he had ever seen or heard about seemed like acts of benevolence. His head throbbed cruelly where the sap had struck it. His vision was distorted and he saw at first through a red haze. He had been gagged so tightly that his cheeks bulged and the nylon stocking they had knotted at the back of his neck drew his lower jaw down and cut harshly into the stretched edges of his mouth. He had been handcuffed behind and strung up by his linked wrists—probably, he thought, by means of a rope thrown over one of the old ceiling beams. He was in a sort of partial suspension, hunched forward, with only the balls of his feet on the floor. The reverse twist of his arms threw his dragging weight full on his shoulder sockets.

But none of this was part of the atrocity. That was on the floor before his very eyes and its victim was—

Kathy! ...

He screamed it soundlessly in his throat and choked on the gag. He wrenched forward, trying to free himself by sheer force, and the pain in his shoulders nearly drove him senseless. It would have been a blessing, but he fought against it and won. He squeezed his eyes shut, momentarily convinced it was all a dream and he could wake himself from it. But when he looked again it was still going on, incredibly, brutally, with a kind of horrible deliberateness, as in some monstrous dissecting room.

Kathy! His beloved Kathy!

His mind refused at first to accept the evidence of his own eyes. But in the end he had to believe, with the fragment of his mind that still clung to reality. Its monstrousness robbed the evidence of all reason, but his eyes saw and his flesh crawled and all of him knew the truth, reasonable or not.

The two fiends, the sudden, unknown marauders, were methodical and silent, except that the tall one, the younger of the pair, emitted from time to time a low, throaty chuckle. He was sweating lightly and his mouth was spasmodically mobile. He breathed irregularly, as in excitement, and this and the periodic eruption of his gross chuckle showed that he got some satisfaction from his work. What he worked with was a straight razor, such as barbers use.

The other, the stocky, paunchy one in the beret, was impassive. Sometimes the light, reflecting from his thick-lensed glasses, gave him eyes like diamonds, cold-white and glistening, a devil's mask. He kept lighting cigarettes.

Mickey had no idea how long it had been going on. But he could see, in one dreadful, endless, too-soon-ended moment, that if it weren't stopped at once, it would be too late. Kathy's eyes had found his. They were wide, straining to reach him, engorged. All of her was in them and he could read the message plainly, the agonized, mute appeal he was powerless to answer.

Rage filled his throat. On the rim of his vision he saw the razor lift and hover. In a final, desperate lunge, he threw himself against the ruthless torque of his binding. He broke both arms and one wrist and tore the ligaments of his shoulder muscles as if they had been strips of paper. Then he fainted, and in that moment Kathy died.

The stocky one dropped a half-burned cigarette. He turned from it, picked up a camera with a flash attachment and adjusted the lens opening. He focused from above, hesitated and muttered something. The tall one, his razor poised, twitched the corners of his mouth.

"Make it look good, huh?" he chuckled.

He stooped, then straightened, and while the other focused his camera again and triggered a blinding flash, the younger one wiped the razor carefully with a small rag, dropped the rag, folded the blade into the handle and slid it into a pocket.

"What about him?" he said.

The two of them looked across Kathy's body at Mickey's sagging form. The stocky one handed over the camera, drew a small automatic from his pocket and sighted. When he squeezed off, the sound was no more than a sharp crack in the high-ceilinged room. The impact of the slug caused the strung-up figure to lurch slightly.

"Get the handcuffs," the stocky one said.

"What?"

"I said get the cuffs! They can be traced."

The tall one went around behind and removed the manacles. Mickey Phillips' body slumped to the floor in a grotesque sprawl.

The two of them prowled the room briefly, looking for other possible traces of their presence. Finally the stocky one bent and retrieved a crumpled cellophane-wrapped cigarette package and put it in his pocket.

"Let's go," he said.

They went out by the front door, pausing long enough to clean the knobs thoroughly. They went down the steps and across the yard to the drive and climbed into a late-model, medium-priced car. The motor came to life, spat once or twice, then settled down and they backed carefully onto the deserted country road.

They had done their job efficiently. Nothing had happened to complicate things; no unforeseen interruptions, no fighting back, not even any back talk. They vanished as they had appeared, in the empty night.

They had made one crucial mistake. They had managed not to kill Mickey Phillips. Mickey Phillips lived and, in the course of time, remembered.

2

For six weeks he lived immobilized in a world of pain and sweat, half conscious. Because of the nature of his injuries, he was encased from neck to diaphragm in a plaster cast, with a cutout over his lower-right chest to permit treatment of the bullet wound. The cast held his arms in flexed position above his chest and was given added stability by suspension from an overhead rigging. The arrangement rendered him helpless to move except from the waist down.

The deadly, endless sameness of his existence was enlivened from time to time, always unexpectedly to him, by brief periods of forced feeding and evacuation; by disturbing inspections and adjustments of his position on the bed; and by a variety of sporadic voices, male and female, that drifted through his mind, occasionally making contact, more often not. What he managed to make comprehensible were snatches of speech, phrases, disconnected fragments.

A man's voice speaking: "... apparently knitting ... those ligaments though ... what's the latest blood count?"

A gentle, woman-voice close to his ear: "Come on now ... just a little ... there!"

A man's voice fading, going away: "... the poor bastard ... oh Jesus, the poor bastard ..."

A conference among men in hushed tones: "... because it don't make any sense; no motive ... if it wasn't for that neighbor woman down the road, probably would have died ... has to be a motive ..."

And another, the voice of a doctor, quietly forceful in the shaded room: "I'm sorry, Captain. If you press him too hard now he may crack permanently. You'll have to give him time."

"Time we haven't got."

"I'm sorry."

It was along in there that he began to emerge from the limbo of that odd, mixed-up world. The process was triggered by two things: first, that the doctor had spoken about his cracking up, and he wasn't ready to crack up—not yet; and second, that he had recognized the other voice as belonging to Captain Andrews, his chief. He had to talk to Captain Andrews urgently. He didn't know exactly why, but he would remember soon and, when he did, he would have to talk to the Captain right way.

Unknown to Mickey, his return to reality was a period of anxiety for the doctors and nurses who attended him. By the marvelous mechanism of repression, he had been protected against the reliving, even the memory, of what had happened to Kathy. But soon now, as he regained physical strength, he could be expected to remember. It was the probable shock of the memory that had the medical people on edge. Their anxiety increased day by day as the nurses reported no sign of shocked realization. One doctor remarked gloomily, "That bothers me more than an explosion. If he goes on and on this way—"

"You think he may develop permanent amnesia, Doctor?" a nurse asked.

"No," the doctor said gruffly, turning away. "I don't think he'll be that lucky."

Mickey lay quietly sweating in the cast, acknowledging by submission to the humiliating hospital routine that he was helpless to care for himself. They fed him by hand, spoonful by spoonful. They bathed him, changed his bed, massaged his legs and as much of his back as was accessible. And they chattered—God, how they chattered! He called them "the jolly girls," and they took it in stride. He hated them passionately, and they knew and were sorry and sometimes miffed, though their studied cheeriness never flagged.

But there was one on night duty who truly helped him, one he couldn't hate, even though her presence in moments of weakness shamed him. When she came, always at night, it was quietly; and she brought peace with her, a kind of tranquil strength, a meaningful compassion.

For some time, he had refused the sedation routinely offered. He pretended he didn't need it, that it upset his stomach. The truth was, he was afraid—afraid of deep sleep, afraid of the Dream. He remembered the Dream and that the Dream was reality. He didn't dare let it return, waking or sleeping, until he was free of the cast and could handle things, take care of himself.

He had developed a system by which he could suppress the memory whenever it arose, gnawing and hateful. He found he could push the horror away into a special compartment. He made of it a caged animal, ferocious but silent, and once he got it locked away he could keep it there as long as he was conscious. He knew it was a makeshift, temporary and precarious; one minute's letdown and it would be free and raging, destroying his sanity. But so far he had been able to keep it caged.

It wasn't hard during the day. There were distractions to occupy his mind, annoying or humiliating though they might be. But the nights were hard and long, when he was alone on the rigorous watch. It was then that the good nurse helped. She would appear unbidden on silent feet, almost stealthily. He would wake from a light, fretful sleep to find her standing by the bed, watching him. She rarely spoke except to ask if she could bring him anything, make him more comfortable. Usually there was nothing to be done, but she would linger on with him, silent and watchful. It was as if there were something secret between them, something timeless, primitive, inexplicable in words.

At times, waking in a cold sweat, fearful because the beast of memory was about to break free, he would feel her hand on his face. She would stroke and massage his forehead and temples, rubbing peace into his mind with cool, dry fingers. These would be the times of weakness. With no conscious warning, he would find himself crying, helplessly, babylike, silently but with tears, and inside he was mush. He was helpless even to wipe the tears away. He had one free, moveable hand, but with his arm imprisoned in the cast, he couldn't reach his face with it. She would do it for him, gently, without comment. She would palm his eyes softly, absorb the wet with the palms of her own hands and stroke his closed eyelids with her fingers.

"Go ahead and cry," she said one night, "I'll never tell."

Somehow he knew she wouldn't, and because he trusted her and because it was time to stop crying and face what he had to do, it was to her he said, "I've got to see Captain Andrews, as soon as he can make it."

"I'll see that he gets the message," she said. "Try to rest now."

When she left that night, it was as if they had said goodbye. He saw her briefly a few more times, but it was never the same with her again.

3

In advance of Captain Andrews' visit, a couple of the men in Homicide came with the mug books. It was a long, tedious job on both sides. It took two full days, and among the thousands of pictures Mickey failed to find the two they were looking for. He knew he hadn't forgotten. He remembered all right. He gave full descriptions in minute detail to the two detectives and again, late in the afternoon, to an artist from the department. The artist worked long and patiently and Mickey sweated it out with him, line by line. When he finished Mickey shook his head. The guy was a good artist. He had come up with two good, professional portraits. But they bore little resemblance to the living faces Mickey remembered.

"Well," one of the detectives said, "we don't cover the whole country. There's millions of mug shots."

They got him on his feet the morning of the day Captain Andrews came to see him. He was appalled at how weak his legs were. He had to be supported to the bathroom and back. But after a short rest he tried again and he could walk all right. It was awkward and oppressive in the bulky cast, but he got around pretty well.

Captain Andrews was a slight, scholarly man with shrewd, probing, gray-green eyes. He didn't fit the stereotype of a veteran policeman, but few of his associates gave heed to stereotypes. The Captain was in charge and there was never any doubt about it, not for a minute. There had never been such a doubt in Mickey's mind, nor was there now, as the Captain looked up from the stiff chair at the foot of the bed.

"You wanted to see me," he said.

Mickey had a few bad moments. This was the boss, a busy man, and he, Mickey Phillips, detective second grade, had actually sent for him! What was he going to say? The Captain didn't have time to sit around and talk about the weather, or make sure Mickey was comfortable and did he need anything.

"Yes sir, Captain," he said. He hesitated a moment, then blurted, "I want to get to work on the case."

Captain Andrews' eyes flicked over the bed and the cast and came to rest on the useless-looking lumps that were Mickey's feet under the bedsheet. Aside from the glance, he gave no sign that there was anything unusual about the request.

"Glad to hear it," he said. "Glad you're feeling better."

"I'll be fine in a few days."

The Captain let that pass.

"What have you got to go on?" he asked.

"Well, for one thing, I figure they were from the West—not East, like around New York. Maybe 'way out West."

"Oh? Why?"

"They had suntans, you know? Deep ones."

"You can get 'em with lamps, Mickey."

"I know, sir, but these looked real, like they spent a lot of time outdoors in the sunshine."

"All right. It's good observation, Phillips. What else?"

Mickey wet his lips with his tongue. He felt the sweat start, cold on his neck and forehead. He didn't know if he could go ahead with it. The explicit horror rose in his gorge, inseparable from the mechanics of its perpetration.

"Well, sir—" he forced it out word by word—"I think the one—the tall one—was sometime a—barber."

"Because he used a razor?" the Captain said quietly, watching.

"The way he handled it—the way a barber learns, you know?"

"It could be," Andrews said carefully, watching the ravaged face of the young, bright, tortured man whom he wanted very much to save, for the force and for his own satisfaction and because he was a human being first and only after that a cop.

Mickey was twisting in the bed and Andrews could see the fine film of sweat on his forehead. He swung his legs over the side and tried to sit up but, overbalanced by the cast, failed to make it and remained sprawled awkwardly, this lean, naked shanks exposed, his face flushed with embarrassment.

Captain Andrews gave him a lift to a position where he could sit in manly fashion and have his pride.

"So, if he was a barber, he probably went to a barber college somewhere, see? And they keep records, don't they?"

"Sure they do," the Captain said. "We'll check 'em all

out, coast to coast. Now let's talk about something else. Motive. That's where you can help the most. Where was the motive?"

Mickey looked at him blankly.

"Yeah, motive. Captain, I've been going over and over it, trying to think of everybody involved in that case. I can't—"

He broke off at the Captain's quizzical look, then blushed hotly. He had certainly dragged that into the conversation, like a poor little kid showing off his only toy. The "Maroney case." The one Mickey had broken, virtually singlehanded, by a combination of circumstance, opportunity, guts and headwork, not to mention some sheer, adolescent heedlessness of danger. The case that had made him a detective second grade while he was still a uniformed patrolman and after less than three years on the force, at the age of twenty-eight. Captain Andrews must have the idea he was going to try and get by on the one case for the rest of his career.

But the Captain only shook his head thoughtfully.

"We checked into that," he said. "Maroney is locked up for at least ten years. He had no underworld connections, no family, no money and no friends to raise it for him. Nobody, in short, cares a damn about Maroney. So there is practically no likelihood that Maroney had anything to do with this—attack."

"I'm sorry," Mickey said numbly. "The only reason I mentioned it—"

The Captain nodded.

"I know," he said. "You're thinking. Keep thinking." After a moment he said, "We've also checked into every case you've had anything to do with. They get us nowhere. I doubt it was a matter of revenge."

"Then what, Captain? What? There has to be a motive."

"Think some more, Mickey. Think 'way back. Did you ever injure anybody? During Korea maybe?"

"No. Hell, I was never in any position to injure anybody—not even the enemy."

"What about—" the Captain hesitated—"What about your wife? What about Kathy?" he asked quietly.

"Kathy? No, Captain. Kathy—she couldn't hurt anybody. She didn't know how."

The Captain had seen a lot of pain in his time, but had never seen the kind of anguish that was in Mickey's eyes at that moment. He turned from it.

"I didn't mean that exactly," he said. "I was thinking of—disgruntled suitors—somebody she dated before she knew you, who might bear a grievance."

He got no answer and when he turned around, Mickey's mouth was moving soundlessly and he was crying. The Captain had to turn from that, too, from the helpless, unmanned bulk, half human, half plaster and wire, like a house with legs.

"Kathy—" he mumbled brokenly, and the Captain would have wiped the tears away, but he knew it would be the worst thing he could do—that the only thing he could do that would be a true service to Mickey was to get out of there and leave him alone.

"Keep thinking, son," he said, picking up his hat. "We'll break it all right, with your help. But you got to take it easy, conserve your strength. So long for now. I'll come back."

He lifted one hand for a parting slap on the shoulder, but held back in time, confronting the bulge of the plaster cast. He was in the doorway on his way out when Mickey said, "Captain …"

"Yeah, Mickey?"

"There's something else. I don't think I told this before. I just thought of it."

"What is it?"

"Another reason I think they're from out West—they talked like it; not like New York or Chicago. Anyway the one did, the young one."

The Captain held his hat very still in both hands.

"From all we could learn," he said slowly, "they didn't talk at all when you could hear them. We didn't know either one of 'em said a word to you."

"Only right at first," Mickey said. "When I opened the door. They were standing out there and the one looked at me and he said, 'Does Mickey Phillips live here?' Then they came in. That's all he said, but the way he spoke the words—it wasn't East—it was like Western—"

He broke off. His head stiffened in an odd attitude above the engulfing cast. He sat rigid. The Captain's scalp tingled. There was a period of almost palpable silence, deep and horrific, like the empty silence of a deep chasm after the screams of the fallen have faded away.

"Captain …" Mickey said softly.

"Yes, Mickey."

"He was looking right at me and he asked if Mickey Phillips lived there. They didn't know me. Or Kathy either. All they had was a name and address. They could get it out of the phone book. They didn't *know*, Captain!"

His voice had risen stridently and Captain Andrews glanced into the corridor. Far down, a nurse was approaching and he beckoned to her. Mickey's voice rode the edge of hysteria.

"It was a mistake, Captain! They got the wrong people! It was all a lousy, stinking, goddamn mistake!"

The nurse reached the door.

"How bad is he?" she asked.

"I don't know. Will you need help?"

"I might."

But Mickey gave them no trouble. The nurse spoke to him gently. He looked at her without recognition; then he allowed her, with Captain Andrews' help, to settle him on the bed and cover his legs. He was no longer crying or sweating. His eyes, fixed on memory, stared past them. Only his mouth moved.

"A mistake," he muttered. "Nothing but a mistake."

On his way out of the hospital, the Captain stopped at a public phone and called into headquarters.

"Start checking out all guys in the city named Mickey Phillips," he said.

Before leaving the booth, he checked personally through the directory. There was only the one Mickey Phillips listed. There were a good many people named Phillips and there were three or four M. Phillipses, but only the one Mickey.

It would be an unbearable irony, he thought as he left the building, if a human life had hung on a telephone listing. And it looked as if Kathy Phillips' life had dangled by that delicate thread.

4

The day after the Captain's visit, they moved Mickey from his private room to an eight-bed ward. There were constant, day-long distractions, but they left him untouched. None of the other patients happened to be a policeman and he felt nothing in common with any of them. He lived in stony silence in the prison of his cast, waiting stoically to be freed.

He attended to some personal business. An administrative officer from the Department came to ask about the disposition of Kathy's body, which had been in storage under county auspices.

"She always said she wanted to be cremated," Mickey said. "I guess that's it."

"The mortuary will take care of the ashes," the officer said, "until you're ready to make some disposition."

"All right," he said.

"We couldn't trace any kin who ought to be notified," the guy said.

"Kathy was an orphan. I think she had an uncle in California."

The administrative officer patted his forehead with a handkerchief and got down to less touchy matters.

"You'll be laid up for a while, even after they remove the cast," he said. "Do you want to authorize someone to enter your house and pick up personal effects?"

"I guess so. Could bring me a suit and a couple of shirts, stuff like that. That's all. I guess my gun's out there—"

"We picked that up. It's at headquarters."

"Then that's all."

"About the house—if you have a payment to make—"

"I'm going to sell the house," he said. "Could you call the real estate guy for me—name is Bert Simons? He could come and talk it over."

"I'll call him."

The real estate man, Simons, was properly sympathetic and briskly efficient.

"All I want is my equity back, in cash," Mickey told him. "I don't want to go out there or have anything to do with it."

"What about the contents—furniture, linens—"

"Sell it—give it away. I don't care."

"Your clothes? And your wife's clothes?"

"Give them to somebody—the Goodwill."

"I'll get to work on it."

"The sooner the better."

He spent four weeks in the ward and finally they came around to remove the cast. He had expected it to be a long, grueling operation, but they had it off in a few minutes. The doctor and a physical therapist checked him carefully for articulation at the shoulders and elbows. He was amazed at how pale and shrunken he was. His broken left wrist was not completely mended and they bound it and made a sling for it, but he could use his right arm and hand at last. There was pain, but after a period of adjustment and practice, he could at least take care of his basic needs. The therapist set up a schedule for him and the doctor warned him to follow instructions and to rebuild himself gradually. He shouldn't expect to go into the ring with anyone the first week.

The therapist was an expert, straightforward and patient, and Mickey respected him. The first few days were agonizing and he seemed to make no progress, but after a week there was noticeable improvement. It was a great day when, for the first time, he shaved himself and dressed, complete to necktie. By the first of September, when they moved him from the hospital to the policemen's convalescent home, his fundamental condition was sound.

He regained strength rapidly now. Within two weeks he was doing restricted, light workouts in the gym. By the end of the month his wrist had mended and he could use more of the equipment, including the light punching bag. He ate heartily and at first he slept soundly and well. Only his spirits failed to keep pace with his physical improvement. More and more often he rejected friendly overtures by the other men. A psychiatrist saw him periodically and was alternately pleased and puzzled after their talks. Mickey was polite, rational, patient and aloof. When he began having the nightmares, he became a problem both to his fellow patients and the staff.

He would wake bathed in sweat, shouting and fighting at phantoms. One or two of the others would have to get up and restrain him. They complained to the head of the staff and there was consultation. A doctor hit on a partial solution. They fixed up a sleeping room off the gym. The therapist, who had an adjoining room, volunteered to stand by. Thereafter when Mickey would wake in the night, cursing and banging on the wall, the therapist would bundle him into a sweat suit, get him to the gym and set him at the heavy bag. For long periods, sometimes till he dropped from exhaustion, Mickey would slash and pummel the suspended dummy. The therapist would lead him back to bed and eventually he would fall asleep.

Whether it was this nightly workout or simply a normal progression, the time came when he no longer had the dream, or if he did, he failed to wake from it. The therapist reported no disturbance for seven nights running.

On a Sunday evening, nearly five months after Kathy's murder, the psychiatrist, who worked part time for the Department, had a long, careful talk with Mickey. At its conclusion he decided that from the patient's point of view, the best thing he could do would be to get back to work. But it was not the psychiatrist's decision alone to make, and late that same night he had another long, careful talk with Captain Andrews.

The next morning, Captain Andrews found himself looking up from his desk at a young man who resembled the Mickey Phillips he had known, but roughly. The features were the same, possibly somewhat leaner, but as he looked more closely, he could see that their effect had changed. The set of the chin, slightly dimpled, had hardened, as if the mouth were steadily, inexorably biting down on something unbreakable; as if it were trying to bite a nail in two.

The lips were thinner, compressed in a hard, pink line. The eyes had an obscured look, as if gauze had been laid over them. They were relentlessly steady and, at a glance, empty, like the glass eyes of a doll. But the Captain knew there was no emptiness behind them; that they looked out of a single-purpose mind. They were the eyes of a man to whom everything had been done.

The Captain shook hands heartily enough and smiled from a sinking heart. He indicated a chair. Mickey chose to stand.

"Good to have you back," the Captain said.

"Yes sir."

The Captain sat back in his chair. He knew what was coming, dreaded it, but he sat like a man and took it—the big question.

"What've we got, Captain?"

The Captain ticked off the elements of their investigation to date. It had not been any tougher for him when the commissioners themselves were on his back.

"We sent out those sketches the artist made from your description; all over the country."

"Any makes from anywhere?"

"Not yet. We checked out everybody named Mickey Phillips in this city and vicinity. Everybody turned out to be you. There aren't any other Mickey Phillipses in town."

He mentioned some other items, but he was talking into the wind and he knew it. Mickey's mouth moved thinly.

"In other words, we've got nothing," he said.

"That's right," the Captain said, "so far."

He took a turn around the desk and sat down again.

"I've set it up for you to run up to Chicago and look over the mug shots. They've got 'em, you know, from 'most everywhere."

When he looked up, Mickey's eyes were fixed on something beyond him. The Captain's flesh crawled.

"Captain, if you please, sir, I'd like to request a leave of absence."

"Naturally, if you're not feeling up to things—"

"A year's leave of absence," Mickey said.

The Captain tightened a few muscles inside.

"It's a wild dream, son," he said. "Give it up."

"I can't."

"What you're asking for is my blessing and the prestige of department to see you through a private manhunt. You know I can't give you that."

Mickey stood mute.

"Listen," the Captain said, "will you think it over? Give it some time—"

"No, Captain—sir."

"I can't give you a leave of absence."

"The Commissioners."

"I'm speaking for the Commissioners!"

"Then I'm resigning from the force, Captain."

Though not strictly comparable, a voluntary resignation from the force was as serious, in the Captain's eyes, as a defection from the priesthood. He watched with rocks in his belly as Mickey Phillips carefully laid his badge on the desk. After a while he looked up.

"I won't argue," he said. "But I'll give you a day or so

to change your mind."

"Long enough," Mickey said, "to look at those mug shots Chicago?"

A momentary hope rose in the Captain like a wild bird.

"As a bargain, son?" he said.

"No sir."

Andrews swung back to the work on his desk that the brief, futile interview had interrupted.

"Then all I can say," he said, "is that the processing takes a couple of days. Your ID will be technically official till then. But if they check with me from Chicago, I'll have to say you're separated from the force."

"Thanks, Captain. Goodbye."

The Captain nodded brusquely, turned over a typewritten sheet of paper and stared at the text till the print blurred.

If it had happened to me, he was thinking. Now, at fifty-five? I don't know. But then—at his age—what would I have done?

Mickey had been in Chicago a few times and could find his way around the Loop. He checked into a small downtown hotel and found his way to the appropriate desk at police headquarters by late afternoon. From a bustling squad room, a plainclothes detective escorted him to a small, well-lighted room, treating him with the respectful reserve a man of action shows for another's tragedy.

"We've got, you know, a hell of a lot of pictures. Uh—you were a—an eyewitness, right?"

"Yeah. There were two guys. I remember them well."

The officer set him up with a couple of the cumbersome mug books, worn and scarred by long use.

"It's a place to start," he said. "If you hit pay dirt, give a yell. We'll start something on it right away."

"Sure," Mickey said.

The officer looked at him curiously for a moment, then opened the door and started out.

"Good hunting," he said.

Pages turned slowly in the big books. Hours passed, shifts changed and Mickey pored over the endless items of the rogues' gallery, face by face, page by page. By midnight, his eyes no longer served him efficiently; one face was like another. He turned in the book, made a note of where he had stopped and returned to his hotel to get some sleep.

He woke before dawn, to the rumble of early morning traffic in the Loop. By six o'clock he was back at the table in the midst of the pervasive hum of the functioning central police headquarters, looking at more pictures. He went back to the hotel at noon, treated his eyes with hot packs and returned to the mug books an hour later. There was little hope left in him that his quarry would turn up here.

He was among the last pages of the last book when the officer who had greeted him the day before came in to see how he was making out. He carried a bulky sheaf of papers in one hand. He shook his head when Mickey said he had had no luck.

"Tough," he said. "You know it's possible they had no

records—"

"I know."

The detective tossed the sheaf of papers onto the table.

"You probably have most of these in your own shop," he said, "but sometimes they get shoved back. Miscellaneous bulletins from all over. I only brought the ones with pictures. Some of 'em go pretty far back, but take a look. These wouldn't be in our books."

"I'll look at them," Mickey said. "Thanks."

The officer studied him.

"How long you been on the force down there?" he asked.

"Four years."

"Well, if you don't find your man right away, don't let it get you down. He'll turn up, maybe when you're not even looking. Most of 'em—nine out of ten—are dumb jerks. They get picked up on a D-and-D, make a fuss, get mugged and there they are and you want 'em for larceny or manslaughter that goes back five years. You'll find 'em eventually; anyway one of 'em, and when you've got him, he'll take you to the other."

"Sure," Mickey said. "I'll find them."

"Good luck," the other said, and he went away.

Idly, almost without interest, as if drained of all expectation, Mickey pulled the papers within eye range and started leafing through the bulletins. They were clipped together at the top and some were so worn and rumpled with handling that the pictures were blurred, the printing smudged, sometimes illegible.

He turned over ten of them, fifteen, twenty,

skimming the dreary catalog of day-to-day crime—
"Wanted for rape, embezzlement, bunko,
manslaughter, armed robbery, grand theft auto, sex
offenses, child beating ..."

He turned to the twenty-first sheet and his throat
lurched as if swallowing a hot wire. He could feel his
heart thumping against the edge of the table. It was
the one—the younger one—the tall one—the one with
the razor. It was unmistakable; the picture was clear,
a good likeness.

His hand was trembling. He depressed the spring
clip, started to pull the sheet out, then paused, left it
in place. This was a personal hunt, no longer a police
matter. It would be nice to have the picture, but he
couldn't risk stealing it from this file.

Hastily, then more carefully, he read the details.
"Wanted for bad checks: Lou Roberts, also known as
'The Barber'; no prior convictions. Jumped bail and
disappeared from local haunts, August 13. Ht. 6' 2",
wt. 190 lbs. black hair, green eyes, mastoid scar right
ear; mole on left cheek. May be working as barber.
Known to consort with prostitutes, suspected procurer;
last known residence, 1318 Bacon Street, Kansas City,
Mo. May be dangerous if trapped."

He read and reread the vital information till it was
as clear in his mind as the face that had haunted him
for five months. He looked at the date of the bulletin
out of Kansas City and groaned. Over a year ago, a
cold, cold trail. But it was something; it was a place to
start.

He went through the rest of the bulletins eagerly
now, half persuaded that because he had found the

one he would inevitably find the other. But there was no face that resembled even remotely that of the thickset man in the beret and glasses.

When he returned the sheaf of bulletins to the officer in the squad room, he affected weary casualness, but he kept his hands in his pockets so the trembling wouldn't show.

"Nothin', huh?" the detective said.

"Thanks anyway, for your trouble," Mickey said.

"Any time. Got time for a cup of coffee?"

"I guess not," Mickey said. "Got to be starting home. Captain will be in a sweat."

"Okay. Take it easy."

"Sure."

He left the building unhurriedly, but halfway down the street and headed for the hotel, he was running. Within half an hour he had checked out and was threading his way through the heavy, rush-hour traffic, southward toward Kansas City.

5

The last address of Lou "The Barber" Roberts was an empty lot, recently turned to rubble, in a frayed downtown section of the city. Because he had to stop (and start) somewhere, he took a room in an ancient, rickety walk-up run by a Mrs. Coral Blake. She was forty, maybe, maybe more; had once been pretty, maybe; and now had the wistful, hungry, big-eyed look of the fading beauty. Overanxious to please the good-looking, strong-looking young man who registered under the name of Joe Marine, she hovered about the narrow, dark sleeping room, fussing over his probable needs. He kept telling her everything was fine, thanks, no, thanks just the same; and finally she left him alone.

The room contained a bed, a chair, a chest of drawers, a washstand and a small closet. A single high window looked out on an air shaft, across which was another window like his, fifteen feet away.

It was midmorning. A raw November wind swirled in the shaft. He had driven steadily, with one or two stops for coffee, for fourteen hours. The small of his back was on fire with tension and his eyes felt exposed and grit-filled. He stretched out on the narrow bed and took stock of his assets and liabilities.

He had something over two thousand dollars in cash, in a money belt next to his skin, the residue from the sale of the house in the country and a few other items. He had enough clothes to get by on. He had a cheap place to stay and the name and a detailed description of the man with the razor, plus the knowledge that Lou Roberts had at one time frequented this neighborhood. He had a medium-priced car, only a year old, in good condition, registered to a man named Mickey Phillips.

The money would steadily diminish and sometime disappear, unless he took steps to replenish it. Mrs. Blake's rooming house would be a good place to live only as long as nobody suspected him of being on the prod. The information he had about Lou Roberts was worthless until he followed through to develop it. The car was a dangerous liability under its present registration. The car would have to go.

He lay quietly, resting, but not permitting himself to doze off, until noon. Then he got up, undressed, went to the bathroom and showered and shaved. He dressed in a clean shirt and another suit and left the building.

He drove the car to three dealers in turn, offering it for cash sale. Each of the three tried to make a trade-in deal with him. The best offer came from the first dealer and he went back there and turned over the car and certificate of ownership and walked out with fifteen hundred dollars. He walked about a mile to a used-car lot and picked out a small, inexpensive European car in good condition. He had to dip into his reserve to the extent of a hundred dollars in order to complete the deal. He registered ownership under the name of Joe Marine and drove back to the neighborhood of the rooming house.

It was a nondescript area of light industry, old residences, chiefly rooming houses, and brick apartment buildings and cheap stores and shops. Scattered among them were taverns with faded, garish fronts. He went into a barbershop, and in the course of a haircut and shave he learned that Lou Roberts had worked in a shop around the corner and in the recent indefinite past had disappeared.

On the street again, he tramped four blocks in four directions, finally asked a storekeeper about Costello's barbershop.

"Out of business," the man said. "Closed up six, seven months ago. Got a Slenderella place there."

"I was looking for a guy named Lou Roberts."

"I wouldn't know. I never went in there."

Mickey drove back to the rooming house, went upstairs and got into bed. His back still ached fiercely; he would be up that night and he had to have sleep.

He woke at six o'clock. The window was black against the air shaft, but there was a light in the room across the way. A young woman with platinum-blond hair was rousing slowly from a rumpled bed. She was nude and the bright light treated her harshly. She pushed herself up with one hand till she was sitting on the edge of the bed. She folded her arms across her midsection, squeezing upward a pair of skimpy breasts. Then she leaned far forward, so that her long blond hair fell across her thighs, and slowly rocked herself as if in pain. After a minute she straightened, stood up, shrugged into a bathrobe and disappeared. A moment later he heard her in the bathroom. Mickey dozed off, and when he awoke again she was dressing slowly, laboriously. He watched her briefly, without interest, then turned away from the light and went back to sleep.

The next time he woke it was much later and there were voices across the way. The shade had been drawn and he could hear the woman's high-pitched giggle and occasionally the lower, guttural tones of the man she was entertaining. It was after ten now, and Mickey got up, washed at the stand, dressed in the dark and went out.

It was raw cold and the streets were empty. He had mapped a tentative route in his mind, fanning out from the rooming house in three directions, and he turned into the first tavern he came to. It was doing a good business, but he found a seat at the end of the bar where it curved to the outside wall. He ordered a bottle of beer and sat with it, drinking it slowly in minute sips, watching, listening.

The crowd was a neighborhood mixture of working people and shopkeepers. It was an unlikely gathering at which to find the shadow of the man he hunted, but he didn't expect a gift from heaven. He nursed his beer and eavesdropped, studying the faces of the eager talkers, listening for a tip, a suggestion, a lead, however slim. He didn't ask questions. Strangers who asked questions were nosy, maybe stoolies, private eyes, even cops. Question time would come later.

Between ten-thirty and the midmorning closing hour he hit twelve joints and learned nothing that would aid his search, but he got acquainted with a couple of apparently friendly and talkative bartenders.

When he returned to his room, as he was putting the key in the lock, the platinum-haired girl came down the hall, singing to herself, a high, off-key, mournful sound. She walked unsteadily, clutching a small paper sack in both hands. As she started past him she swerved, careening into him. He caught her with one hand to steady her. She looked up at him, breathless.

"Oops," she said. "Dark in here."

She burped, looking at him, then smiled with small, not very good teeth.

"Parm me, honey," she said. She held up the sack, still smiling, weaving a little from side to side. Except for the teeth, she wasn't unattractive. "Come on in, honey, have a drink—on me." She giggled. "I mean the *drink* on me, I mean— Huh?"

"Sorry, not tonight," he said.

She pouted, backing off.

"What's a matter—you some kind of a social worker, or something?"

"No, ma'am. I'm just tired."

"Oh. Well, okay. I'm tired too. Very tired. G'night, honey."

Inside, after he had got ready for bed, he sat on the edge of it for a while, staring at the drawn, yellowly lighted shade of her window. Part of the description of the wanted man had read, "Known to consort with prostitutes." Likely a pimp among other things. If this girl hadn't known Roberts personally, she might very possibly have known about him She might be a lead.

But cultivating prostitutes, or any sort of woman in the world, was a project for which he had no stomach. There were dark memories still too near the surface— devilish, lurking memories of a brief radiance swallowed up in ugly blackness. As the sight of her nakedness earlier had failed to stir him, the thought of trying to make friends with her, of touching her, repelled him almost to the point of nausea. Not because she was a whore; because she wasn't Kathy; because Kathy couldn't be ...

Lying in bed, waiting for sleep, he let himself remember Kathy, alive and whole; all of Kathy, her vibrant, urgent flesh against his ...

He remembered crying at the memory of her and was surprised that he now could remember without crying.

After several days of making the rounds of the taverns, moving in a widening arc around the neighborhood, he realized it was too random a process. Also it was expensive. He would have to find a way to make some money, and the time to start was before his reserve ran out. A man who didn't need work was more likely to find it than one who did.

He found what he was looking for under the heading, "Schools, instruction, trade schools."

"Bartenders!" the ad read. "Make steady pay with big tips. Our intensive training course union-approved. Apply now."

Every bar was a listening post. When a man went to work behind a bar he automatically became a confidant to the general and specialized public. Depending on the location, he might pick up a lot of information. Besides, having a trade and a union card would keep him in pocket over an indefinite period.

He went to the school to apply for the course. It would take three weeks, six hours a day, and would cost a hundred and fifty dollars in installments, or a hundred twenty-five in advance. When he paid the whole thing in advance, the head instructor said he could probably complete the course in two weeks if he had any aptitude.

He had the aptitude and he was in a hurry. The principal instructor and his wife, who assisted him, were conscientious and thorough. The classes were small. He learned what was involved in operating on a percentage. He learned the state liquor control laws by heart. He learned how to take care of a bar, how to wash and clean glasses, how to prepare garnishes and setups. And he learned how to mix a vast number of basic highballs and cocktails and something about their variations. He passed his "final exam"—a grueling, two-hour practice stint under simulated working conditions—with flying colors.

The instructor's wife signed his certificate and congratulated him on his achievement. If she could make one suggestion, she said, it would be that he might try to smile a little more often. Mickey said he would take it under advisement.

It was snowing lightly by the time he got back to the rooming house that day. He had brushed his feet on the mat and started up the stairs when the door of the manager's apartment opened and Mrs. Blake looked out. She came to the banister and gazed up at him with her big, lonely eyes.

"You doing anything special tomorrow, Thanksgiving?" she asked.

"I guess not," he said.

"Nobody ought to be alone on Thanksgiving," she said. "Why don't you come down and have dinner with me? I'm having a few people in—just from around the house. Turkey and all the trimmings."

"Well—sure, all right, thanks," he said.

"Come early," she said. "We'll have some cheers before dinner."

"All right."

He was surprised at himself when he got to his room. The manager's apartment was the last place he wanted to spend any time. But he decided he might as well go. It would be a free meal and there might be some people there who could help him.

Early on Thanksgiving, he went out and bought a bottle of whisky, so he could make a contribution to the party. When he knocked at her door, Mrs. Blake opened it herself and he saw at a glance he had made a mistake in accepting the invitation.

She was all dressed up in a strapless party dress that had probably been quite a number in its day. But now it was too short and a little too small for her and she had to keep hiking it up to keep her breasts covered. They jiggled and floated precariously at the top of her bodice, like filling leaking out of a couple of cream puffs. He could tell by the fragrance of her breath and the look in her big eyes that she had several drinks already and there was a glass in her hand as she let him in.

"Hurry up, honey, and get yourself a drink," she said. "You've got to catch up."

"Well, I don't know," Mickey said, "I'm not much of a drinker."

"Oh come on," she said, slipping her arm under his. "It's a holiday!"

In the kitchen he could smell the turkey and there were things in pots and pans on the small stove. There were gin and whisky on a shelf and he made himself a drink while she bustled about unsteadily. He saw that a table in the dining alcove was set for two.

"What about the others?" he asked.

"Others?" She blinked. "Oh, they couldn't come. So I decided we'd just have it—tête à tête." She giggled into her glass.

She nearly lost her balance, seating herself on the living room sofa and he had to catch her arm.

"Come on, honey," she said, "let's start living it up—before we get any older."

He raised his glass halfheartedly. He was embarrassed for both of them. He wished he hadn't come and he couldn't think of anything to say to her. Not that it was necessary to say much.

There was a row of photographs on an old-fashioned sideboard across the room. They formed an irregular rank, ill-assorted and variously set forth, some in easels, some mounted on cardboard. There were several small children among them, a typical family array.

"Lots of pictures," he said, pointing.

She blinked slowly, clearing her vision.

"Oh, family stuff," she said. Her face brightened. "I got two girls, both married now. One married at seventeen, the other at eighteen. Good-looking girls. We had the first one a couple of years before the war and he got me pregnant again just before he left." Tears glistened in her eyes. "I never saw him again," she said. "I mean after he went away."

He tried to feel with her the remembered pain, but couldn't make it touch him. Getting killed in a war—you could expect to get killed. It wasn't anything like the monstrous murder of Kathy. Besides, it was old, long ago.

She dragged him into the kitchen again for another drink. He made himself a very light highball and tried to lighten up on hers, too, but she happened to be watching at the moment, so he went ahead and made a normal-size drink. She picked it up, leaned over to look into the oven and almost fell in. He caught her at the waist and she leaned against him with excessive gratitude.

"You're strong," she said. "You just saved me from a fiery death."

She linked arms with him again, and when they got out of the kitchen he steered her to the sideboard where the pictures were lined up. There were more of them than he had seen from across the room, some half hidden behind others. Some were unmounted snapshots.

"Tell me about the family," he said. "Which are the married daughters?"

"I don't know," she said, pouting. "You'll find out I'm a grandmother."

"You're the youngest grandmother I ever saw."

That mollified her and she pointed out the members of the family one by one, with a few earthy side comments. When she turned from the shelf, she lost her balance and fell back against it. Some of her drink slopped out of the glass.

"Whoo!" she said, fanning herself with her hand. "I'm a little tighty-tight, huh?"

She brushed at her hair and hiked her dress up. He looked away from her, gazing idly at the pictures. There was a snapshot of a young man, stuck behind one of the easels. He could see only enough of it to see it was a man. He reached across the shelf and pulled it into view. His throat squeezed shut convulsively. He forced air through it, then took a quick sip of his drink and glanced at her. She didn't seem to have noticed. He held the picture around where she could see it. It was a picture of Lou "The Barber" Roberts.

"Who's this?" he asked.

She looked vaguely at the snapshot, then got it in focus and her face twisted savagely.

"That," she said between her teeth, "is a certain son of a bitch I once knew."

She glared at the picture, her big breasts lifting and falling spasmodically.

"Take it away," she growled. "I don't want to look at it."

She turned away and Mickey slid the picture into his pocket.

"He give you a bad time or something?" he asked.

She looked at him with the fierce concentration of the foundering drunk.

"What would you know about a bad time?"

"Try me," he said.

"You are looking at the number one sucker of the neighborhood," she said. "This guy—can you believe it—took money from me! *Money* I gave him."

She swayed, clutched at the sideboard for support.

"You know what he did with it?" Her eyes groped and found him. "The son of a bitch took it upstairs and gave it to that little twist up there, that Irene. You must know Irene by now, don't you? She must have been around to see you by this time."

Her glass slipped from her hand and fell to the floor. She kicked at it, sending a spray of watered whisky into the room. Then she turned to him, her hands out, reaching, and when she started to fall, he caught her. She swayed against him, clinging to his shoulders, crying in earnest now.

"Oh, baby, honey," she sobbed, "I wouldn't have to give you money, would I?"

He could feel her flesh damp under the tight dress. The tears had streaked her make-up.

"Well," he said, "what happened to him? He just walk out, or what?"

"I don't know what the hell happened to him," she sobbed. "I know what I hope. The hell with him. Listen, honey, take me over there and set me down, will you? I got to sit down and I don't think I can make it by myself."

He slipped his arm inside hers and started across to the sofa. She made it for three or four steps, then collapsed and fell heavily to the floor. He knelt, got one of her arms around his neck and lifted her. She wasn't as heavy as he had expected. He put her down on the sofa and smoothed her dress over her knees. He looked at her for a moment, then pulled off her shoes and set them on the floor. There was a folded patchwork quilt at the end of the sofa and he covered her with it and went out to the kitchen. He turned off the oven and the top burners on the stove, then tiptoed out of the apartment, making sure the door was locked from the inside. He turned up his collar, went outside and walked till he found a small restaurant, a bar and grill. He had dinner and a couple of bottles of beer. When he got back to his room, it was dark.

He put the snapshot of Lou Roberts in his money belt. He didn't spend much time looking at it. He didn't like to look at it. The room was stuffy and he opened the door and sat on his bed in the dark. He was sitting there when the light went up in Irene's room across the air shaft. After a minute he heard her door open and the faint slap of her slippers in the hall. There was a pause and he heard the slippers again, padding closer. She came to his door, peered inside, took a step into the doorway, then saw him and jumped, startled.

"Hello, Irene," he said.

"Hi."

She settled back against the doorjamb, looking toward him. She was wearing a sheer negligee and the light from the hall filtered through it, outlining the casual contour of her still-young, still-marketable body. She yawned widely, covered her mouth with the back of her hand as an afterthought. The gesture had a pathetic elegance.

"No place to go?" she said. "I just got up."

"Uh-huh," he said.

"Me neither," she said. She shifted to the opposite side of the door, exchanging one jutting hip for the other. "You had dinner or anything yet, honey?"

"Yeah," he said. "I just got back."

"Oh. I was just going out. I'm starved."

"There's not much open tonight."

"It's always like that, Thanksgiving and Christmas."

"Everywhere the same," he said.

She yawned again. She shifted her position three or four times in the lighted doorway.

"I hate to eat alone," she said finally.

"Yeah," he said.

She lingered another half minute, then sighed, ran her hands upward through her hair, lifting her breasts in profile against the light.

"Well, if I'm going, I'd better get started," she said.

"I guess so."

"So long, honey."

She started away, then turned back in a burst of quick irritation.

"You bug me!" she said petulantly. "What's wrong with you? Don't you ever get *lonely?*"

"Sometimes," he said.

She glared at him, then turned, swishing the robe about her ankles, and stalked away to the bathroom. After a while he got up and closed the door. He stretched out on the bed, locked his hands under his head and looked at the ceiling. He didn't feel lonely. He felt tentative. He felt like a man waiting.

6

He did some waiting for a job to turn up, dividing his time between the union hall and a couple of downtown employment agencies. The union sent him out on two temporary jobs, one an afternoon shift in a large commercial hotel, where he spent most of the time washing glasses and preparing setups. The other was a private party at a country club. He worked from five in the afternoon till around three in the morning, but it wasn't too bad because all he had to do was to serve drinks and not bother with tabs or handling cash and making change.

He continued to read the papers, scouting the personals and want ads for both leads and jobs. He did a lot of leg work, up and down the winter streets, making a systematic canvass of barbershops and nearby cafés and hangouts—any place that in the remotest likelihood might produce a lead to Lou Roberts.

The damp snow weather had passed and the air was dry and cold. It braced him, but he was on edge, restless, longing for some kind of action. He had given up making the rounds of the taverns, because it had got him nowhere and he didn't want to spend the money. Besides, he felt his best lead so far was right there in the rooming house, if only he could find a way to develop it without drying up the spring of information. He hadn't seen Mrs. Blake since the Thanksgiving "tête-à-tête." He had thought about going to see her, to pump her about Roberts, but he was pretty sure she wouldn't talk about it when sober, and drunk, she was, to put it mildly, undependable.

Neither had he seen Irene since the night she had come fishing for an invitation to dinner. He suspected it would be more difficult to get information out of her than from Mrs. Blake, but he knew the time would come when the way would open.

It came sooner than he had any right to expect—on a cold, windless night in early December. As usual, he was sitting in his room, in the dark, waiting, stolid and patient, as if he were suspended motionless while the world moved about him, near him, all around him, but not touching him.

At ten-thirty he heard footsteps in the hall, a man and a woman, and recognized the tone of Irene's giggle.

They passed his door and a moment later the light went on in her room. The shade was only half drawn and Irene made no move to pull it down. There was nothing unusual in this; sometimes she did and sometimes she didn't.

Her client was a well-dressed man of middle age who was in a state of drunkenness bordering on stupefaction. He handed her some money, which she laid on a nightstand near the bed. Then she tried to put him off, apparently in the hope that he would pass out and forget the terms of their transaction. But he wouldn't be put off and finally she submitted, not bothering to undress beyond the essential minimum. The procedure required about three minutes and Mickey found himself elaborately disinterested. At its conclusion, the man, with alcoholic extravagance, opened his wallet and dangled a piece of currency.

Irene played it coy, lowering her eyes modestly; then without waiting too long, raised her skirt and permitted him to stuff the bonus into the top of her stocking. He gave her a pat and weaved out of the room. Mickey heard him going away and downstairs, and then it was quiet again. Irene went to the bathroom, returned and sat on the bed, attended to her manicure and brooded.

Ten or fifteen minutes passed and he heard footsteps approaching again, heavy, masculine, not drunk. There was some knocking and Irene got up to let him in. It was a younger man than her recently departed customer. He was heavy-set, bulky in an overcoat and a low-brimmed hat. The collar was turned up and

Mickey could see little of his face.

He said something to her and Irene stood aside and gestured toward the money on the nightstand. He counted it, put some of the bills in his pocket and left the remainder. Irene watched him sullenly. He said something more and she shook her head and shifted her nail file to her left hand. The man spoke again and she shook her head stubbornly.

He seized her wrists, twisting till the file fell from her hand. He had bent her backward and she was staring up him, shaking her head. Her mouth worked as if she was cursing him. He pushed her down onto the bed and she kicked at him. He pushed her dress down and made a search about her stockings. It didn't take long. He found the hidden currency and put it in his pocket. He straightened and spoke to her and Irene kicked at him with both feet. He pushed them aside, leaned over the bed and struck her three times across the face, right, left and right again. She rolled slowly onto her side and buried her face in her arms. The man started out of the room.

It looked like the break he'd been waiting for. Mickey reached for his coat and hat and stood at the door, listening to the heavy feet going away. They started down and he counted the steps to the first landing. Then he left the room quietly and went after him, buttoning his coat as he went.

At the top of the stairs he waited, peering down the switchback of the banisters. When the guy was two full flights down, Mickey went on down himself. He heard the front door of the building open and close as he turned down the last flight toward the ground floor.

Mrs. Blake's apartment opened, and she slid into the hall and leaned beside the door watching where the guy had disappeared. She didn't look at Mickey till he started past her.

"What'd he do, beat her up again?" she snapped. "She probably asked for it, sucker."

"You know his name?" Mickey asked, his hand on the doorknob.

She just glared at him.

"Men!" she said, and she made a spitting mouth. "Chasing after a dirty, chiseling bitch like her. When a good man could have it for free if he had any sense."

"Yeah," Mickey said. "If I run into a good man, I'll let him know."

He got outside, moving quickly now, crowding the shadows of the entry as he headed toward the street. The guy was walking away to Mickey's right, toward the deserted corner half a block away. A heavily bundled couple, male and female, passed and Mickey left the entry and got to the sidewalk behind them.

His man turned right at the corner. The screening couple was moving fast and Mickey paused in the shelter of the abandoned store front in the corner building and looked around. If the guy had a car handy, he would have to do some running to get back to his own and get it going.

But the subject was still walking, faster now. The entire neighborhood was closed down for the night and Mickey remembered an alley midway along the block. He moved around the corner and went on at a shuffling trot, closing the gap between them. His rubber-soled shoes made no sound on the dry concrete.

When they reached the wide-mouthed alley, they flanked it, one at each corner. The bulky one hadn't looked around.

"Hey, you," Mickey said, and moved diagonally into the alley.

The guy stopped, stood stiffly, his head swiveling cautiously.

"Don't look around," Mickey said. "Just back up around the corner. You're covered and, man, I'll drop you, believe me. Now back up in here."

There was a moment of hesitation, then the pimp grumbled, "Okay, take it easy."

He backed slowly till he was clear of the brick building that formed one wall of the alley.

"In here," Mickey said.

Uncertainly, the big guy backed into the shadows. Mickey grabbed the collar of the overcoat, jerked hard and swung him against the wall, moving out in the same moment to pin his arms to the brick. The impact knocked the guy's hat off and Mickey could see him all right now. He wasn't anybody familiar. His face was gross-featured and, at the moment, fearful.

"What the hell—?" he said.

"I want the dough you took off Irene," Mickey said.

"You're nuts—"

Mickey slapped him with the back of his hand. The guy's head snapped and he went off balance. Mickey straightened him up.

"Okay, okay," the guy said. "It's not worth it. You want me to get it out or you want to feel around for it?"

"Go ahead," Mickey said, "get it out. Just the money."

He released the arms, stepped back a little but stayed within reach. The guy reached into his pocket and paused, looking at Mickey's open hands.

"Some guts," he grumbled. "You ain't even heeled."

"Try something," Mickey said.

"Okay, forget it."

His hand came out and there was a bill in it. Mickey gestured impatiently.

"Come on. The one you took out of her stocking. Don't pull that switch on me; I'll make you hurt for a month."

"Listen, it was only a twenty."

"Get it up."

The guy reached into his overcoat pocket and brought out another bill.

"Just toss it over there," Mickey said, nodding. He flipped the bill to one side.

"I didn't know Irene had a boyfriend," he said.

"You got the wrong lead," Mickey said. "I'm no boyfriend. I'm taking over."

"You're what? You're nuts! I been working this string for a year."

"I don't want the string. Just Irene. I figure I can make her into something."

"Make her into what, for crissake?"

"I got an attachment for her. See, I sort of inherited her from Lou Roberts."

"Roberts. That schnook? He's been gone from here forever. You been suckered."

"Maybe. You got the message now? Don't come around Irene. She's mine."

"You can have her. She ain't worth the trouble it

takes to climb the stairs."

"Pick up your hat," Mickey said. "You can go now."

The guy leaned down warily and picked up his hat.

"Hey," he said, "you said you inherited her from Roberts. What happened to him?"

"Nothing. He's living it up, like always."

A short, throaty laugh.

"Living it up—in Denver?"

Mickey said nothing.

"Well, good luck, sucker," the other one said. "Tell Irene goodbye for me."

"Get going now, huh?"

"Yeah, sure."

He put on his hat, hitched up his coat and turned away out of the alley. Mickey scooped up the bill and headed back to the rooming house. Mrs. Blake was not in sight when he got there.

He went upstairs and knocked on Irene's door. There was a long pause. Then he heard her voice close to the door.

"Who is it?"

"It's me. Joe. Joe Marine."

"Who? Oh. Well, what do you want?"

"I've got something for you."

A pause.

"I'll bet you have."

"Something that belongs to you," he said. "Money."

After a moment he heard the bolt slide back, and the door opened. She had undressed and was wearing the sheer negligee again. Her feet were in worn pumps with rundown heels.

"Well?" she said.

He pushed inside, closed the door and leaned against it.

"What happened?" she said dully. "You finally get hungry?"

He held up the twenty-dollar bill. She looked at it cautiously, ran her tongue over her lips.

"What's it for?" she asked.

"It's yours. A guy gave it to you and another guy took it away from you."

Her eyes narrowed.

"You go around doing good or something?" she said.

"It's the same bill. I got it from the guy who took it from you."

"You what? Off Patsy? You're crazy!"

"So I'm bringing it back."

She reached for the money.

"All right. It's mine. Give it to me."

He held onto it.

"I will. But I want to know something."

Her shoulders slumped. She turned away, sat down on the bed and rubbed her face with her hands.

"Okay," she said wearily, "give me the hook. What do you want, the story of my life?"

"Just part of it," he said. "The part about Lou Roberts."

Her head lifted slowly and she made a face—a bad face. He thought for a second she was going to be sick.

"What about Lou Roberts?" she said.

"Well, I heard some things about him. I'm trying to get in touch with him."

She looked at him for a long time.

"Get out of here," she said. "Go on. Blow."

He shrugged, stuffed the money into his pocket. "Maybe I had the wrong dope," he said. "I understood you knew Lou Roberts."

She was sitting stiff and straight on the bed. Her hands clutched her knees so tightly that the knuckles were pale.

"Yeah," she said, "I knew Lou Roberts."

She rose to her feet. Her hands fumbled at the belt of her robe. She gathered the front panels in both hands, opened the negligee and faced him.

It was on her middle belly. It was clear enough—an L-shaped pink scar, forming an incomplete frame for her navel. It had been cut skillfully, deep enough to scar, not deep enough to destroy. It would be a thing for a girl to remember.

She looked down at herself almost curiously.

"Guys see that, you know," she said. "'That's pretty cute,' they say. I tell them it stands for love."

She closed the robe and sat down on the bed.

"Do you know where Roberts is now?" he asked.

"No," she said. "I don't know."

He laid the twenty on the nightstand.

"Okay," he said. "Good night."

He had got his coat off and was hanging it up when she knocked on the door, a flurry of small fists beating. He opened up and she came in, reaching for him.

"Listen," she said, "you got that money from Patsy, you would have to beat the hell out of him. What'd you do? Is he dead?"

"No, he's not dead."

She swayed against him, pushed back, ran her hands

through her hair and leaned against the wall, shaking her head.

"Oh God," she said, "you dumb jerk. Now what? He'll come back. He'll lay for me."

"Now take it easy—"

"Take it easy! What do you know around here? Girls have got killed for less than what you did—"

"Don't worry about Patsy. He won't be back."

"Oh, he won't be back, huh? They always come back. With their big dirty hands and the stinking cigars— they come back. With acid they come back—with knives—razors—"

He took her arms and shook her gently. Her long platinum hair swung about her face. She showed her bad teeth at him.

"Let me go! You got me killed. That's not enough?"

"Listen to me," Mickey said, holding her. "Patsy is chicken. I stacked him up against the wall. He wasn't even bruised. I asked him for the money and he gave it to me. That's how tough Patsy is."

"You're not a girl!" she yelled.

She put her face against his chest.

"Oh God!" she said. "Oh sweet Jesus! The guys I run into!"

She felt fragile in his hands, like a thin stick that would break in two if he didn't let go. There was an unpleasant smell about her, the smell of fear. She was shaking spasmodically and he thought she wasn't putting it on. She was really scared.

Of course, he thought, she might just be cold in that skimpy bathrobe....

Suddenly she pulled away and threw herself on the

bed. After a minute, Mickey went to the closet, took down his suitcase and opened it on the bed beside her.

"Oh God!" she was moaning. "Oh God, what'll I do?"

When he didn't say anything, she raised herself and stared at the suitcase.

"So you're going to run out now?" she said.

"Not exactly."

"Boy, you fixed me good."

He was packing hurriedly now and he let some time go by before he said casually,

"Then maybe you'd better go with me."

"Go—where?" she said.

"Like out West," he said.

Her eyes showed some interest.

"Las Vegas?" she said hopefully.

"Maybe, in due time."

"Where first?"

"Denver," he said.

"Denver!" She frowned petulantly, her lower lip outthrust. "My God, you really looking for Lou Roberts?"

He stared at her. She put her hand to her mouth.

"So you knew he was in Denver. How come you didn't tell me?"

She pouted.

"I didn't want to get mixed up in anything."

"You don't have to get mixed up in anything. But you can help me find him. I'll make it worth your while."

She chewed her lip, calculating.

"If I go to Denver with you," she said, "when you get

through there will you take me to Las Vegas?"

"Maybe. I won't make a deal on it."

"Then I won't go."

"If you don't go," Mickey said, "I'll find Patsy and tell him I changed my mind. He can have you back."

"You dirty rat!"

"Suit yourself," he said.

She sat up and hugged her knees to her breast.

"When are you going?" she asked.

"As soon as you're ready."

"All right."

She got off the bed carefully.

"Need any help with your suitcase?" he said.

"I haven't got a suitcase."

He took his own off the bed.

"You can use what's left of mine," he said.

He went with her to her room and put the suitcase on the bed. She was shrugging out of the negligee when he went out. He wrote a note to Mrs. Blake, reminding her that his rent was paid up for an extra week and saying he was sorry he couldn't give her more notice. When he looked across the air shaft, Irene was replacing the cap on a half-pint bottle of whisky. He went back in there and closed the suitcase. There was a cheap, brown fur coat lying on the bed.

"Is your rent paid up?" he asked her.

"Sure. So what?" she said.

"How much do you owe Mrs. Blake, up to today?"

"Nothing!" She looked at him, "Well, around ten dollars, I guess."

"How much?"

"Twelve-fifty," she muttered.

"Have you got it?"

"Maybe."

"Then leave it here."

"Leave it! Are you nuts? It'll just get stolen."

"Even if it does, you'll know you left it."

"I will not! That old hag has been making life miserable for me for a year."

"Then give her a good belt sometime. But leave the money."

"You gonna make me?" she said belligerently.

He took a step forward and she grabbed her purse from the bed, opened it, grumbling, and dug into it. She got out some bills and laid them on the table. He went over and counted them and said,

"Another buck and a half."

"Oh Jesus!" she said. "How did I ever get mixed up with you?"

She slapped down another dollar and a half and thumbed her nose at him. He held the fur coat for her while she got into it, which wasn't easy because the lining was ragged and got in the way.

"Got everything?" he said.

"Yeah, I got everything. Let's blow this crummy mausoleum."

He didn't care for her choice of words and said nothing as they went downstairs, Irene clinging tightly to the banister. They got past Mrs. Blake's door without incident and out onto the windy street. Irene yanked her collar up around her face and swore softly.

"Denver!" she growled in disgust.

Mickey put the suitcase in the back seat of the little car and Irene stared at it, aghast.

"In that?" she said. "All the way to Denver?"

"It's not far," he said. "Get in."

She bumped her head getting in and swore some more. He got the door shut and went around to the other side. He started the car and pulled away.

I hope he's still there, he was thinking. Let him be there!

7

They were approaching Denver late in the next afternoon, when she tossed him the big question. It was cold, but the sun had been out all day and there was no wind. There was snow on the mountains to the west, but the fields and roads were clear and dry. They had eaten a hearty lunch and by four o'clock, Irene had fortified herself at the whisky bottle and was in a talkative mood.

"What've you got with Lou Roberts?" she said.

"I just want to find him. I've got a deal for him, a business deal."

She snorted.

"With Lou? He only knows one kind of business— mine." He didn't say anything and she looked at him with moody suspicion.

"I don't know if I like this," she said. "You going to operate something with Lou Roberts? Like call girls or something?"

"Nothing like that."

"You better watch your step," she said. "You already took me across two state lines. There's a law against that."

"I know," he said. "You going to turn me in?"

"Well, you just watch it."

"Irene," he said patiently, "I brought you with me because I thought you could help find Roberts. You don't have to stay. If you want, we'll find the airport and I'll buy you a ticket back to Kansas City."

"How can I go back there?"

"I don't know."

"How about a ticket to Las Vegas?"

"All right."

On the southern fringe of the city, he stopped for gas and in her hearing, asked the attendant how to get to the airport. He wrote out the directions meticulously, and when he left the station he took the charted course. Irene said nothing until they had traveled several miles and were passing airport markers frequently. Then she shifted on the seat and moved close to him, slipping her hand under his arm.

"Listen, Joe," she said, "let's not go to the airport right away, huh? It's just—well, you're so damn quiet-like, and I don't know anything about you and, I mean—why wouldn't I worry a little?"

She laid her head against his shoulder and he could smell the whisky on her breath.

"You be good to me, Joe," she said, "and I'll be good to you. Okay?"

He turned then and began working his way downtown. By seven o'clock he had checked them into a commercial hotel where the rooms were clean and the rate reasonable.

When they were alone, Irene kicked off her shoes,

stretched out on one of the twin beds and left it to
Mickey to open the suitcase and put its contents away.
He had planned to take her downstairs for dinner,
but when he saw the condition of her wardrobe he
decided to have it sent up. As a matter of practical
necessity, she would have to have some new clothes.
It appeared to be up to him to buy them.

During the meal, largely silent because Irene had
wanted to go out and was pouting, he cast up his
resources mentally. On reserve in his money belt he
had about fifteen hundred dollars. There was no need
for Irene to know anything about that. He would start
looking for work the next day, but he couldn't count
on anything immediately. He could invest in Irene to
some extent and it was likely she would have to be
strung along with a series of modest bribes. The
hungrier he could keep her, within limits, the more
likely she would be to hustle around on his behalf. He
could dangle Las Vegas like a promised toy before a
child.

After dinner she decided to take a bath. When she
had left the room, he took off the money belt, emptied
it and put it on a shelf in the closet. He took a hundred
out of his pool and added it to what was in his wallet.
The remainder he put in one of the hotel envelopes,
sealed it, wrote his name and room number on it and
took it down to the desk for safekeeping. While he
was down there, he bought a newspaper.

When he got back to the room, she was still in the
bath. He could hear her splashing and singing in her
high, thin, off-key voice. He got on the bed with the
newspaper and started through it item by items, line

by line, as had become his custom. He had reached the want ads when Irene came in. She was, as usual, naked, and when he glanced at her over the paper, she was inspecting herself in the full-length mirror attached to the bathroom door, turning this way and that, pinching herself here and there, muttering.

By the time he finished the paper, she was getting into her negligee. He looked at it with distaste. In the rooming house it had seemed to fit, but now it looked sleazy and cheap.

"You need some new clothes," he said. "We'll get some tomorrow."

Her face brightened.

"I sure do," she said.

She looked into the closet, then turned to him slyly.

"Especially," she said, "I need a new coat."

"I can't buy you a coat," he said. "Maybe a cloth coat if we can find a good buy."

"A cloth coat! Listen, if you expect me to make it with high-class guys, where the money is—"

"A cloth coat!" he said firmly. "If you have to have a fur coat, too, we can get this one cleaned and repaired. It will have to do."

She flounced on the bed, pouting.

"You're cheap," she said, "like the rest of them. Like Patsy. If a guy has ten dollars—take it."

"I'm not expecting you to make it," he said, "with high-class guys or any other kind."

"What am I gonna do, sit around all day?"

"What I want you to do," he said, "is to get acquainted with some of the local girls and get a lead on Lou Roberts. That's all you have to do."

"Man," she said bitterly, "if I could get to Las Vegas—"

"We'll talk about Las Vegas later."

She sat upon the bed, reached for a bottle of nail polish and began giving herself a pedicure. There was a telephone directory on the stand between the beds and he went through it idly, for lack of anything else to do. There were a lot of people named Roberts, but no Lou Roberts.

Irene moved over to his bed and sat on the edge of it. She put her hand on his knee lightly.

"Honey," she said, "I'm sorry I was bitchy. I didn't mean it. I appreciate what you're doing for me, I really do."

"It's all right," he said. "You'll be helping me, too."

"What kind of a deal do you want to make with Lou Roberts?"

"I'll tell you sometime. I don't like to talk about it in advance. Bad luck."

She put her hand on her abdomen. There was a far-off look in her eyes.

"He wasn't such a bad guy," she said, "in some ways."

Mickey put his hands under his head and looked at the ceiling. Irene went back to her own bed. After a while, he got up and went to the bathroom to get ready for bed. When he came in, wearing pajama trousers but no top, she was lying on her bed, watching him. He sat down, facing her, and stretched, yawning.

"Hey, you're really built, Joe," she said. "Some big physique."

He reached for the light switch.

"What's that?" she asked, pointing to his chest. "That little scar there."

"This? Nothing much. I fell on a stick."

"Fell on a stick?"

"That's right."

He turned off the light and got in bed.

After a couple of minutes, Irene said, "Fell on a stick. What a way to get hurt!"

He ran his hand over his chest, probed at the small, drawn scar under his ribs.

Which one of them did that, I wonder? Roberts, or the other one—the one in the funny hat?

I'll know pretty soon now. Let it be soon!

He woke early in the morning and dressed quietly so as not to wake Irene. He left a five-dollar bill and a note reading, "I'll be back by noon. Here's money for breakfast and lunch in case I'm late. We'll go shopping this afternoon."

He reached the headquarters of the local union at nine o'clock. It took him about an hour to get lined up and eligible for local work. There were no jobs that the union knew of that morning.

He stopped at a downtown employment agency. They were dubious because of his limited experience, but they let him file an application.

Next he went to the local office of the barbers' association and asked if they had an up-to-date list of employed barbers. A woman at an outer desk looked him over carefully.

"Well—yes," she said, "we have such a list."

"I'm trying to locate—a friend."

The word stuck in his throat, but he managed to get it out. The woman shook her head firmly.

"We can't release that information," she said.

He didn't stay to argue. Time was a crawling thing on his back. It was like shooting at the moving targets in a gallery. You hit what you could and went on to the next.

He did some preliminary window-shopping, trying to figure out what it ought to cost to outfit Irene adequately, without too many frills and within his budget. He arrived at a rough estimate for everything, including a cloth coat, of around three hundred dollars.

The hotel room was cluttered and stuffy. He could hear Irene singing in the bathroom. He opened a window. On a service cart were the remains of a large, half-finished meal. There was an open quart bottle of whisky on the bedside stand. The level was down by perhaps two ounces.

He recapped the bottle and pushed the service cart out into the hall. He was sitting on his bed, gazing moodily at the bottle, when Irene came from the bathroom, rosy-skinned and jiggling.

"Hi, honey!" she said. "Did you find a job?"

"Not yet," he said.

"Well, that's all right. You will. You can always get a job around Christmas."

She moved around the room in casual nudity, chattering. He caught sight of the L-shaped scar on her belly and it gave him a bad feeling in his stomach.

"Put some clothes on, huh?" he said.

"In a minute."

She had got into a tight, somewhat padded brassiere and a garter belt and was drawing on her hose when she said with commercial coyness, "What's the matter, honey? Does it bother you?"

"Where did you get the bottle?" he asked.

"I had it sent up," she said defiantly.

"Signed for it?"

"Sure. They let you do that—"

"Don't do it anymore."

She snapped into her immediate pouting fury. "Now listen, you—"

He raised his hand to stop her.

"It's not that I want to change your habits," he said patiently, "but it costs too much that way. Buy it in a store and bring it up—all right. But go easy on the room service."

Grumbling, she pulled a dress over her head, let it ride her hips while she adjusted it above.

"Some big shot," she muttered.

"I'm not a big shot," Mickey said, "but I'm the big shot in your life at this time."

"I can do better!"

"You just let me know when you've made the connection," he said.

She glared at him a moment, then turned her back and went to the dressing room to comb her hair.

This shopping tour, he thought, is going to be rugged.

He looked at the bottle for a minute, then reached for it and twisted the cap off. He lifted it and drank from it. It burned his throat and mouth, a good counter-irritant in his mood, but it felt bad when it hit his stomach.

The shopping was less rugged than he had

anticipated. She was amenable to suggestion and accepted his approval or veto with fairly good grace. Only once did she turn on him, whispering desperately, "Do you have to look at the price tag on everything?"

"Yeah," he said. "I do."

When they came to the coat that he had found and priced earlier, and Irene took off her sleazy, worn fur, the saleslady barely managed to refrain from wrinkling her nose. Irene noticed, and Mickey thought for a moment they were going to do battle.

"Listen, honey," Irene said, glaring at the woman, "if you got any smart cracks to make—"

Then Mickey stepped in and smoothed it over, and Irene calmed down. While she tried on the new coat, Mickey asked the saleslady where they could find a good place to have the old fur reconditioned. She stroked it reluctantly and asked, "What fur is it?"

Irene swung around.

"It's genuwine Missouri jack rabbit," she snapped, "and it keeps me real warm, honey."

The saleslady gave them the name of a fur-cleaning establishment.

"It's a very nice coat," she said, swallowing with difficulty.

"You're damn right," Irene said.

Mickey got her out of the store and they walked to the fur shop. He had ordered everything sent to the hotel and Irene was anxious to get back there. He was relieved that she didn't want to spend the rest of the day in a booze joint.

As they crossed the hotel lobby, a paunchy man in a wrinkled suit angled to intercept them at the elevator.

He had a lady's glove in his hand.

"Mr. Marine?" he said pleasantly.

"That's right," Mickey said.

The man looked at Irene, smiling, and dangled the glove, "Found this on your floor," he said. "I wondered if it might belong to you—uh—Mrs. Marine."

Irene stared at him a moment, took the glove and looked it over.

"Just one you found?" she said.

"Yes," the guy said.

She handed it back reluctantly.

"No," she said. "It's not mine."

"Well, thought I'd ask. I'll put it in the lost-and-found department."

Mickey pushed the elevator button.

"Enjoying your stay with us, Mr. Marine?" the guy said.

"Sure," Mickey said. "It's a nice hotel."

"Good. Well, I'll see you around."

He wandered off into the lobby and they got into the elevator. Mickey pushed the button for their floor.

"Hey, that was pretty nice of him, huh?" Irene said.

"He's the hotel detective," Mickey said. "He was just sizing us up."

"Oh? How do you know?"

"I've seen it before. It's an old dodge."

"You mean, like he wonders if we're really married?"

"Not exactly," he said.

The room had been made up in their absence. The bedspreads were neat and smooth; the rug had been swept and the ashtrays, formerly filled with lipstick-stained butts, been emptied. Irene took off the new coat and tossed it on a chair and started at once to open a package of lingerie and hose. Mickey hung up the coat. When he returned, she was holding up a pair of black, bikini-type panties.

"Pretty cute, huh?" she said. "Want me to model for you?"

When he said he had to go out again, she pouted and threw herself on the bed.

"What shall I do," she said, "just lay around the damn room all day, all night—?"

"Just try to relax," he said. "Try on your new clothes and I'll take you some nice place for dinner."

"It's about time," she said.

"Yes," he said. "It is."

As he left the room, she was lighting a cigarette. He hoped she wouldn't burn down the hotel.

With the nearest corner to the hotel as a checkpoint, he started a tour of barber shops in the downtown area. In the first, he got a haircut. There were only four chairs and none was operated by Roberts. The next three he visited were busy, with customers waiting, and he sat down and waited long enough to make sure Roberts wasn't there, then left, saying he couldn't wait any longer. In the next shop, he went for a shave. Noting the fresh haircut, the barber looked at him oddly, but made no comment. A couple of places farther along he found a shoeshine stand and let the boy do a job on his shoes while he looked the place over. By closing time, after dark, he had hit fifteen shops with no result except that his tonsorial condition was good.

After buying the clothes for Irene, he had only a few dollars left in his wallet and he stopped at the hotel desk for his envelope, took another hundred out of it and returned it to the clerk. His reserve was diminishing. He hoped a job would turn up soon.

He had his key out and was about to open his door when someone called to him softly. He looked down the hall and it was the house detective, beckoning from the back stairway. He went down there. The detective led him out to the landing and pushed the heavy door to. He had the bland, pleasant look on his face.

"I hate to bring this up," he said, "but I thought I better tell you first; you'll know how to handle it."

"Handle what?" Mickey said.

"Well, the fact is, we had a little problem with your—uh—wife this afternoon."

"What kind of a problem?"

"Well, she evidently became somewhat—intoxicated. She was a little noisy."

"All by herself?"

"Yeah, Mr. Marine. I had to ask her to quiet down. Like I said, it's not too serious, but the management runs a quiet place here and if they get complaints, then I have to do something."

The blandness in his face had hardened into a set smile.

"Something like what?" Mickey said.

"Mr. Marine, I'd hate to see you and—your wife—thrown out. You're nice-looking young people and—"

"I'll speak to her about it," Mickey said and turned away.

The hell with that, he thought, heading for the room. I've got no money to spend putting in a fix with some cheap hotel dick. We can always move.

When he went in, Irene was sitting in the armchair in her black panties, doing her nails.

"Hi, honey," she said, without looking up.

Her bed had been opened and was badly rumpled. The ashtray on the bedside stand was overflowing. Some of the butts had lipstick on them and some didn't. The level of whiskey in the bottle was down by three or four ounces. He saw that he wouldn't have to worry about putting in a fix. Irene had taken care of that.

"I'll take a shower and get dressed for dinner," he said.

"Okay, honey."

When he returned to the bedroom, she had made no move to get dressed. He sat on the bed to put on his shoes and socks.

"We going to start looking for Lou Roberts tonight?" she said.

"Maybe. If we can make some contacts."

"Look," she said, "I don't know anything about Denver—like where the girls hang around or anything. Every town is different. You have to be careful."

"Just do the best you can. Maybe this hotel detective can help. He's a good friend of yours, isn't he?"

There was quite a long silence. He heard her get up. The bed lurched slightly and she was sitting beside him. She slid her arm over his shoulder.

"Joe—honey—I had to," she said with quiet urgency.

"Listen—he came in here, no knock, no nothing. He's got a key. All I had on was a pair of pants—"

"It's all right."

Her hand stroked at his head and neck.

"I didn't know you'd care, Joe. You never said anything, never touched me. If you care, honey—"

"I don't care."

"Well, see, he started hinting around like there was something—wrong, about us. He said he might even have to throw us out of the hotel. It was only for you, really, not for myself."

"Yeah. How did he put it to you?"

"What do you mean?"

"I mean what did he offer?"

"Oh, well, he said if he could come up and see me once in a while, maybe he could straighten things out, you know? I told him I didn't know what you would do, you might kill him—"

He looked at her sharply.

"I might kill him? Why would you say a thing like that?"

"I had to say something. After all, we're registered here as Mr. and Mrs."

"Okay."

"That's all there was to it, Joe, honest. It didn't mean a thing to me. It was just so he wouldn't throw us out."

He sat brooding over the disheveled bed. She lifted his hand, laid it against her naked breasts.

"Joe, baby—"

"Did he ask any questions?"

"Like what?"

"Like what are we doing here?"

"No. He—"

"Did you happen to mention anything about Lou Roberts?"

"No, I didn't." Her voice took on an edge of calculation, the old we're-in-this-together tone. "I wouldn't do that. I know you don't want anybody to find out you're looking for Lou Roberts."

He disengaged his hand, laid it flat on his thigh and spoke slowly and distinctly.

"That is right," he said. "Because some other people know about this deal and I have to get to Roberts first, before things get loused up."

He gave it a chance to register.

"You understand that, Irene?" he said.

After a moment she said casually, "Sure, Joe. Whatever you say."

He forced himself to a gentler manner.

"All right. Let's get dressed and go out on the town."

As she got up, he slapped her buttocks in a friendly way, saw her smile privately, turning her head away. He had no idea how much she had put together in her erratic little mind, but he knew that the longer it took him to find Lou Roberts, the more risk he would run with her. For a few dollars she would put herself in anyone's hands, and his own dollars were dwindling.

They were leaving the room when the telephone rang. He felt momentary shock, until he remembered he had left his number with the union and the employment agency. He went back between the beds and picked it up. It was somebody at the union headquarters.

"We got an emergency call for a substitute at a small joint near downtown. The regular man has to leave on account of a death in the family. He'll be gone about a week. You want a week's work?"

"Sure," Mickey said. "Where's the place?"

"Write it down." The guy's voice gave him the address and he wrote it down. "The employer is a guy named Fenelon. Girard Fenelon. Got it?"

"I got it."

"How soon can you get there?"

"How soon does he need me?"

"No later than ten o'clock."

"I'll make it."

"Okay."

He joined Irene at the door and they went out.

"What was it?" she said.

"A job," he said.

"Oh? Starting when?"

"Ten o'clock."

"Tonight?"

"We'll have dinner first."

"What kind of a job is it?"

"Tending bar."

She looked at him quickly.

"I didn't know you were a bartender," she said.

"What did you think I was?"

"I don't know."

They were alone in the elevator, and after it started down she laughed shortly to herself.

"You know what I really thought you were?" she said. "Some kind of a cop."

"Oh? What made you think that?"

"Oh I don't know. Sometimes you act like it."

He was glad to have the information. It was something to watch in himself.

8

Girard Fenelon was a small, harassed-looking man with a graying mustache that twitched in spasmodic response to an irregular tic in his left cheek. He owned two spots; not that he expected to get rich, he explained to Mickey, but it was well to have insurance. If you happened to make a little on one joint, you needed another to pay the taxes. He realized that bartenders also were unlikely to get rich. He was sympathetic about this, but felt called on strongly to advise there wasn't much he could do about it personally. No bartender was going to get rich at Fenelon's expense— on the side, so to speak. In other words, he ran a clean joint on a strict percentage and no bookmaking, pushing, B-girls nor procuring would be tolerated.

He closed the brief orientation lecture with a measured pause and a philosophical sigh.

"Even if I should be tempted, my wife would never stand for it. My wife, Mr. Marine, is an excellent woman."

As it turned out, Mme. Fenelon did not visit the bar during the time he was there and the problem never came to a head. Fenelon was easy to work for. The hours were long; Mickey had to be there at four in the afternoon to get ready with the setups and didn't get off until two in the morning. But he got an hour's dinner break between seven and eight, and Mr. Fenelon, who divided his time between the two taverns, usually managed to relieve him for short breaks two or three times in the evening. A cocktail waitress came on for the cocktail hour, stayed until seven, then returned at nine, so he didn't have to worry much about table service. The clientele was quiet and congenial and not too demanding. The first few hours of the first night were nerve-racking because of his limited experience and the long gap between his training and the actual work situation. Making correct change quickly was tricky until he got the hang of it. Also, he found himself stumped on several orders. But Mr. Fenelon, who was there most of that night, hovering about him like a worried mother hen, took a liberal view. He showed Mickey a reference file under the back bar where he could find the recipe for nearly every drink known to man.

"Nobody can remember some of those crazy drinks," Fenelon said. "Don't worry about it. Just look it up so they won't send it back."

It was nearly three in the morning when he got back to the hotel. Irene, fully dressed except for her shoes, was lying on her bed, smoking.

"How did it go?" he asked casually

He was more eager for the information than he let himself show. He had left her on her own soon after dinner.

"All right I guess," she said, shrugging.

She eyed him, stretched herself lazily on the bed,

letting her skirt ride high on her thighs. She gazed at him, almost curiously, then rolled over slowly, turning her back to him.

"Unzip me, will you, Joe? I can't reach."

He leaned over her, found the zipper tab at the back of her neck and pulled it down. It was a plain but chic wool dress and the fabric had a softly nubby texture under his fingertips. The dress parted in a deep, narrow V, revealing part of her rather good back, the long, straight, faintly corrugated line of her spine.

Without turning, she reached back awkwardly with one hand, scratching in relief. After a moment her fingers plucked futilely at the fastening of her bra.

"Come on, honey," she pleaded softly. "Help."

He slipped his fingers under the tight band and unhooked it. Her flesh was warm and vibrant to his touch. She sighed deeply, snuggled face down into the bed.

"Ah," she said, "my poor, aching back."

Without conscious impulse, only half aware of what he was doing, he ran his fingers slowly along her spine, massaging the tense vertebrae and tiny knots of muscle on either side. She stirred, wriggling in appreciation.

"You ever-lovin' doll," she murmured. "You ought to be one of those—you know—a masoose. What good is a bartender?"

"Did you make any contacts?" he asked.

She grumbled incoherently.

"What?" he said.

"I said nothing much. I met a few people—a couple of the girls." She giggled, a muffled sound in the wadded pillow under her face. "A real big man in a white cowboy hat tried to pick me up, but I turned him down." She twisted her head and looked up at him with a mischievous squint. "I didn't think you'd like it," she said.

"Anything else happen?"

"Not much. I didn't find out anything about Lou Roberts, if that's what you're hinting at."

"Well," he said, "you can't expect everything all at once."

He had stopped massaging her and was sitting beside her on the bed. She rolled onto her back and pushed up on her elbows, her hair in disarray, her half-bared shoulders and upper arms imprisoned in the girlish dishabille of her new dress.

"You know," she said, "you're a sweet guy, Joe, a real sweet guy."

She held out her hand and he helped her to sit up. He found himself looking at her newly, almost with tenderness. Something in him responded to an unsuspected warmth in her. For the first time since the trauma of his personal tragedy, he felt erotic stirrings.

She sensed it. Smiling, she touched a forefinger to his lips, returned it to her own, then repeated the gesture in reverse. Watching him with half-closed eyes, she slipped her arms from the sleeves of the dress, one at a time, holding the bodice up as a shield until both hands were free, then pausing a moment longer, teasing, before she lowered it, pushed away the unhooked bra and exposed little by little her high, stunted breasts with their small nutlike nipples.

He leaned toward her, somewhat off balance. She smiled again, flexed her left knee and drew back her skirt to uncover the top of her stocking where her supporters clutched it. She waited for him to loosen them, her eyes urgent with suggestion.

And the thing died in him. Only feebly stoked to begin with, the slight flame sputtered and went out, choked by some damper whose source was as vague to him as the earlier ignition—some defect in her performance; a too precise timing, an overexplicit purposefulness in her gestures; an exposure of the classic art of the temptress, as if a faulty spring in a window shade had caused it to roll up unexpectedly; a blatant revelation; some or all of these closed down to shrivel the blaze of that momentary bonfire. Or something deeper, in himself, an intuitive recognition that possession on her terms was a double-edged sword and that her blade, if she chose to wield it, was more destructive than his because of their different goals.

Irene stared at him with a kind of horror as he got to his feet and slapped her knee lightly.

"Come on," he said. "You're a big girl now. You can undress yourself."

"You—" Her mouth twisted, struggling for words. "You're not normal!"

"I guess not," he said, turning away.

From that moment, she began to be afraid of him. Mickey didn't realize it at first. She realized it only vaguely herself. But she realized that he had rejected her ultimately, and rejection bred subtle retaliation.

They saw each other, waking, only for brief periods after that. They led separate lives out of the same headquarters, lives that rarely touched. When he woke, around ten in the morning, Irene would be asleep and he would dress quickly and go out to press his systematic search for a clue to Roberts' whereabouts. It carried him farther day by day as he worked from downtown into the outlying districts. He would return to the hotel in time to dress for work. Irene would usually have gone out; if not, she would speak to him only if necessary. He had given her the address and telephone number of Fenelon's tavern, but he never saw her there nor heard from her. Once, she had left the hotel before he went to work and didn't come in until six the next morning. She was helplessly drunk, and he had to undress her and put her to bed. She lost consciousness during the process. He was looking for a nightgown or pajama top, because she had a tendency to get uncovered while she slept and he didn't want a pneumonia case on his hands, when he found an assortment of soiled hose and lingerie stuffed into a dresser drawer. He realized she hadn't done any laundry and she had no clean underclothes left. He put everything in the lavatory and left it to soak. She could decide for herself whether to wear it or tend to it.

On the morning of the last day of his employment by Fenelon, he woke and lay quietly, lingering, his hands linked under his head. After a while he got up and dressed, went down to the hotel coffee shop for breakfast and afterward stopped at the desk. He paid their bill to date and checked himself out.

"My wife will stay on for a few days. If you'll give me the single rate, I'll pay it in advance."

The clerk told him the rate and he paid a week's rent for her.

"I'm leaving money with her, of course," Mickey said. "She can pay cash for anything else she needs. Simpler that way."

The clerk gave him a receipt for the advance rent. He went up to the room and Irene was still asleep. He got his suitcase and packed what he had. There were some things with the hotel laundry service and he called to have the sent up. After a few minutes, a boy brought them. He was putting them in the bag when Irene woke up. He heard stirring, but went on with the packing and closed the bag before he looked at her. She was on one elbow, blinking.

"Going somewhere?" she said.

"Yeah," he said. "Time to move. I'm not getting anywhere here. I think Roberts has either gone back to Kansas City or has moved on, maybe west."

"What about me?" she said.

"Your rent is paid here for another week. If you decide not to stay, they'll give you a refund."

"You promised to get me to Las Vegas."

"Not exactly," he said. "We had a kind of bargain, remember?"

He waited a short time and she didn't say anything. He went to the bathroom to make sure he hadn't left anything

When he came back, she said, "What about your job? You running out on that too?"

"This is the last night," he said. "It was a temporary

job."

She flopped onto her back and yawned deeply. He picked up the bag and started out. When he looked back, she uncovered her left leg, raised it high in the air and was stroking it lovingly with both hands.

In the hall he met the house detective.

"Checking out, Mr. Marine?"

"Yes," Mickey said. "Mrs. Marine will stay on for a few days."

"Oh. Well, we'll take good care of her."

"I'm sure you will."

He got in the elevator, pushed the button for the next floor down, and when he got there, reversed direction and returned to his own floor. He left his suitcase in the hall and walked quietly back to Irene's room. He could hear her voice raised in angry protest, a shrill curse, the sound of a slap. He put his key in the lock silently, turned it, opened the door and went in.

Irene was crouched, naked, on the bed, as far back from the edge as she could get. The hotel detective was leaning over her, one hand raised. She spat at him.

"Stay away from me—you stink!" she hissed. "You make me sick to my stomach!"

"Don't give me that, you cheap tart—"

Mickey moved between the beds and grabbed the detective's left arm. He spun him half around, hit him hard in the midsection, then snapped his head back with a short, lifting blow to the chin that rolled him back on to the other bed and off to the floor. He was around the bed by the time the detective had scrambled to his feet. When he saw Mickey poised, the fight went out of him. He straightened his jacket with one hand and nursed his jaw with the other.

"I don't know if you need this job or not," Mickey said, "but we can fix it for you to lose it. Now stay the hell out of here."

The detective rubbed his neck gingerly, turned and walked out of the room. Irene was sitting on the edge of the bed, leaning forward with her arms folded tightly over her stomach.

"I don't think he'll bother you again," Mickey said. "If he does, call the hotel desk."

"All right, Joe," she said dully.

He waited a short time, but she said nothing more and he went out. He picked up his suitcase and went downstairs. His car was in the hotel garage and he hung around there while they filled the tank and checked it out for him. Then he put his suitcase in the tonneau and drove out to the street.

He drove about a block and a half, found a place to park the car, locked it and walked back to the hotel. From a doorway across the street he could watch the coffee shop and main entrance. He waited till after two in the afternoon, when finally Irene went into the coffee shop. She ordered a big meal and dawdled over it until nearly three. He waited doggedly, moving about frequently, stamping his feet against the cold.

She came out of the main entrance, looked in one direction, then the other, finally turned toward the principal shopping street to her left. Mickey followed on the other side of the street. She wandered the streets for about an hour, window shopping. She turned into one store and came out a few minutes later with a small package. After a while she went into a café and had a cup of coffee and some ice cream. At four-thirty she turned into a hotel bar called The Pony Ring. Mickey went to the lobby and found a spot from which could look into the dimly lighted cocktail lounge.

Irene sat alone at the thinly populated bar, nursing a long drink. From time to time the bartender would pause opposite her and they would talk, sometimes with laughter. A customer moved from some distance to sit beside her and bought a round of drinks. Pretty soon Irene was shaking her head firmly, persistently, and the man finished his drink and went out. Mickey watched while three others approached and tried to pick her up. She turned them all down.

He was deeply depressed. His hunch hadn't proved out. He had come to believe in his own mind what he had told her earlier—that Lou Roberts was no longer in town. There was nothing to do but start again, try to pick up the trail. Irene had outlived her usefulness.

It had begun to snow and he turned his collar up for the walk back to his car. It snowed softly, in large, wet drops. It muffled the city sounds, created a pseudo silent world of wet black pavements. When he reached the car, its small, curving top bore a fluffy white cap, like frosting on a cake. He got in and started it, and drove slowly over the darkening street, to Fenelon's tavern.

Mr. Fenelon was glad to see him. It was a Saturday

and he looked forward to a good night. The first half of the evening met his expectations nicely. The place began filling up early and by nine o'clock there wasn't a vacant seat at the bar and most of the tables were occupied. Still, for Mickey it wasn't a backbreaking grind. It occupied his mind and kept him from brooding. The cocktail waitress was cooperative and uncomplaining. By the jingle of her pockets every time she approached the bar, Mickey decided she was making a good thing of it.

Fenelon came back from the other place at nine-thirty and gave him a fifteen-minute break. He had to leave again at ten, by which time the crowd had leveled off. By eleven it had begun to thin out. The standees around the bar disappeared gradually, and by eleven-thirty there were vacant stools and the volume of sound had diminished. The booths and tables held fairly steady and when Fenelon returned at midnight, he was well pleased.

In the next half hour the tables began to empty, the cocktail waitress took a break and Fenelon decided to check the cash and get back to his other spot. Mickey had a small cluster at one end of the bar and not much else to worry about. Fenelon was seated at the cash register and Mickey was washing glasses when the front door opened and Irene came in.

He held his breath, wary of the condition she might be in. She was wearing the new coat and there was a damp film of melting snow on her shoulders and collar. She stood near the door, looking around nearsightedly until she spotted Mickey, then shook her coat back and moved toward the bar. He breathed a sigh of relief at her steady carriage.

She sat down and laid her purse and gloves on the bar, shook out her hair and ran her fingers through it.

"Hi, Joe," she said.

"Hello," he said.

Silence had fallen at the cash register and Mickey saw that Fenelon was gazing at her steadily with a firm, set expression.

Mickey nodded casually.

"It's all right," he said. "It's my wife."

Mr. Fenelon's face smiled in relief.

"Didn't know you were married, Joe."

He came down from the register and beamed at her across the bar.

"Irene," Mickey said, "this is Mr. Fenelon, the boss."

"Glad to meet you, Mrs. Marine," Fenelon said heartily. "I was just thinking what a good thing it's been for me to have your husband working here. That's a good man you've got."

Irene looked a little startled.

"I guess he's all right," she said. "You shouldn't tell him right to his face, though. He might get stuck up."

Fenelon laughed.

"I'll watch that," he said. "Make yourself at home, Mrs. Marine."

He returned to the register. Irene took out a cigarette and Mickey lit it for her. They were midway along the bar and had it pretty much to themselves.

"Well," she said quietly, "you must be a pretty good bartender, huh? Make me something."

"What'll you have?" he asked.

"Let's see—I think I'll have a champagne cocktail with a needle of cognac, you know—"

"Come on," he said. "How do you want the whisky?"

"Raw," she said. "It's cold outside."

He poured her a shot and set it down, along with a glass of water. She sat over it, gazing moodily into the back-bar mirror. One by one the customers went out, calling, "So long," or "Good night, Joe." Fenelon completed his checking, stuffed into a moneybag all the cash except a small amount of change and closed the register.

"Good night, Joe, Mrs. Marine," he called.

Irene waved her cigarette at him.

"Good night," Mickey said.

A few minutes later the cocktail waitress came in from the back and looked the place over. She was looking Irene over when Mickey said, "I can handle it, if you want to take off."

"I guess so, Joe. Thanks."

She went away. One couple remained in a booth near the door. A man at the bar stolidly finished a lonely bottle of beer, got up and went out. Irene leaned on both arms on the bar, flicked cigarette ashes into the empty shot glass and inhaled, squinting as the smoke curled upward about her face

"I just dropped by," she said, "to tell you—I found out where Lou Roberts is."

9

Mickey's hands shook as he went on cleaning up. His throat was dry and stiff. For a few minutes the room to which he had become accustomed went strange around him. His heartbeat had stepped up sharply.

He wasn't prepared for such a violent reaction. He felt like a man who had forgotten when he first boarded the merry-go-round, only to be brought up short when it stopped and there was the brass ring, dangling within easy reach.

Irene pushed her shot glass across the bar. Mickey washed it and filled it for her, slopping over a little and cursing under his breath. She watched him with quiet curiosity. To escape it, he went out into the room and made a tour of the booths and tables to make sure they were clean. He paused at the booth near the door to announce last call for drinks. It was a young couple, and the girl looked up at him vaguely. Her escort said hurriedly they didn't want anything more.

By the time he got back to the bar he had regained some control. The realization had struck him that Irene might tell him anything, if only to hang onto her meal ticket another day, a week, a few hours.

He washed the few glasses he had picked up and put them away. He watched impatiently by way of the mirror, waiting for the young couple to leave so he wouldn't have to put them out. A minute and a half before the deadline, they obliged. He went to the front door, locked it and switched off the outside lighting. When he turned back to the bar, Irene had swung around on her stool and was sitting with crossed legs, the upper one swinging slowly back and forth.

"Don't you want to know where he is?" she asked.

"Sure, if you want to tell me."

"That was our bargain, wasn't it?"

"I guess it was," he said.

"You better make sure, Joe, because I decided I don't want to get stuck in this town."

"I'm sure."

"Well, he's living in a little town sort of up in the mountains—not too far, about fifty or sixty miles."

"What's the name of the town?"

She dropped her cigarette on the floor, wriggled down off the stool to step on it, then wriggled her way back onto the seat.

"It's not exactly a town, I guess. It's like a ghost town. Nobody lives up there in the winter, except there's this hotel. It's a place called Laurel Flats. They had a gold rush there once."

He started away toward the back room.

"Where you going?" Irene said.

"To get my coat," he said.

In the rear service area he hung up the white jacket, got into his own and his hat and overcoat. He checked the lock on the back door, turned down the thermostat and went back out front.

"How about one for the road?" Irene said.

"It's after hours," he said.

"What? Who in hell would know the difference?"

"Mrs. Fenelon," he said. "Let's go."

She got down, grumbling, and joined him at the door. He turned off the rest of the lights and checked the bolt on the door. His car was parked on a side street and they walked over there and got into it. The snow had stopped, but it was colder and it took him a while to get it started. Irene looked around once at his suitcase in the back seat, but said nothing.

"What would Lou Roberts be doing up in the mountains all by himself?" Mickey said.

"Well, he's not exactly all by himself. See, this hotel is owned by some woman—"

"Oh."

"And that's her home, so she stays up there all the time."

He got the car started, let it warm up for a while, then drove slowly out from the curb and headed downtown. "How long have you known this?" he asked.

Irene shrugged. "What's the difference? I'm telling you now."

"But why would you hold out on me?"

"You held out on me!" she said defiantly.

After a minute he said, "Yeah, I guess you could call it that."

"But I changed my mind," she said, "after that thing with that lousy hotel detective—that dirty—"

"Where did you get the dope on Roberts?"

"Some girl told me. She went around with him when he first got in town, about three months ago. He tried to pull the same thing on her he did on me—you know." She touched herself down where the scar was. "But she got pretty sore about it. She was even going

to call the cops. So Lou ducked out and she said that's
when he went up to the mountains, to this hotel. There
was an ad in the paper. She didn't know where he
was at first, though. Then she ran into him one day
and he told her. They kind of patched it up about
the—cutting thing. She never did tell the cops."

There was slush on the quiet streets and it was
freezing gradually. He drove carefully, pulled up
opposite the hotel entrance. Irene sat toying with the
door handle.

"You want to come up for a while, honey?"

"Not tonight."

"Well, what're you going to do? You going to see
Lou?"

"I don't know. Maybe. Maybe I'll give him a phone
call, see if he's interested in this deal."

"About our deal—for Las Vegas—"

"After I talk to him," he said. "I'll be in touch with
you."

"Well, where are you going to stay? Like tonight I
mean?"

"I'll check in somewhere. I have to think over some
things. Mr. Fenelon wants me to go to work at his
other joint."

"You going to?"

"I don't know yet."

"Don't you want to go to Las Vegas with me?"

"Maybe. We'll see."

"Joe, tell me the truth. You got another girl? Are
shacked up with somebody?"

"No."

"Honest?"

"Honest. Come on now, run along and get your sleep. I'll call you."

"Tomorrow?"

"Or the next day. For sure. Now beat it."

"All right, Joe. You be careful." She opened the door and got out, her feet cautious on the slippery walk. She leaned down to look at him. "Don't stand me up, Joe."

"I won't stand you up."

"So long, honey."

He nodded as she slammed the door. He watched her across the street and into the hotel, then pulled away,

On a through highway at the edge of the city, he found a gas station open. While he was having the car serviced, he got out a map and studied it. Laurel Flats was a tiny dot about sixty miles to the southwest. There was one sizeable town, from which the road to Laurel Flats angled away from the main highway.

"How are the roads?" he asked the attendant.

"They're clear, the last I heard, as far as Boulder."

Mickey thanked him and paid for the gas.

"Going skiing?" the attendant asked.

"Not this trip."

"Well, take it easy."

He drove southwest on dry, clear roads. There was no traffic aside from an occasional truck. There was some snow banked along the sides of the road and he slowed down for depressions where moisture had gathered and frozen. After an hour, he pulled in at a motel with a lighted sign. It took a few minutes to rouse the manager, with whom he left a call for six o'clock. He took a hot bath, shaved and went to bed for two hours. He slept restlessly off and on, but when the call came, he was wide awake and waiting.

At seven o'clock he had breakfast in a roadside café outside of Boulder. It was a cold, quiet Sunday morning. The sky was clear overhead, but clouds were massed over the mountains rising beyond the town.

A few miles beyond Boulder, a road twisted up into the mountains and ended a short distance beyond Laurel Flats. On the map, it appeared to be a fifteen-to-twenty-mile climb. Four miles beyond where he sat at the moment, the map showed a crossroad from the highway over to the main road out of Boulder northwest. He continued along the highway, watching for the crossroad. It turned out to be a narrow country road with some snow banked along the shoulders and spread white but shallow over the flat fields on both sides. It had looked level when he entered it, but after a while he realized he was climbing steadily, though gradually. After a few miles, the once flat fields changed to low, rolling hills. There was snow on the road now, but it was hard-packed and rutted and the car rode it safely. Overhead and behind him, the clouds were high and soft and a thin sunlight warmed the car at first. Then as he approached the inner highway that wound along the base of the high western plateau, it grew darker, colder.

The canyon road was wide and looked clear as he started the climb, but he had no idea what it would be like farther up. He made good time at first. There were patches of snow, but on the lower, gentler grade, he rolled over them easily. It was clear and fast for half a dozen miles; then the road narrowed, the grade steepened and he could feel the small car laboring in the climb. There was more snow, and now and then he lost traction and would have to slow down and shift to low gear to keep from skidding off the edge.

The road dropped off abruptly on his left. Across the canyon, at more and more frequent intervals as he climbed, he could see the half-obscured entrances to long-abandoned mine shafts dug into the mountainside. Against the background of the erratically drifted snow, they were incomplete squares of black timbers framing the blacker holes. From one, near the bottom of the canyon, narrow-gauge tracks curved out of the shaft and a couple of snow-laced ore cars stood empty and derelict. Farther on, in a deep, man-made cut, a huge mine shed reared, rusted and peppered with jagged holes in the iron sheeting that formed its walls. He passed an isolated frame building perched on a ledge above the road, a long-unused schoolhouse.

As the road neared the summit of the climb, it broadened again and the grade leveled off. The rock-strewn cliffs gave way to rolling, open meadows with clumps of trees here and there. The snow had a deceptively leveling effect. Underneath, he felt, the terrain would be rugged and tortuous.

The road straightened and he drove half a mile to its end, where it formed a junction with a crossroad that stretched away in both directions over the high plateau. There was a marker, half-buried in snow. He got out to brush it clear. The sign read: "LAUREL

FLATS—2½ MILES." He glanced up the road and it was clear as far as he could see. A quarter of a mile ahead, it rose sharply, then dipped into a densely wooded area.

He swung into the road toward the wood plot. He found it dense on both sides, except for clearings at intervals where cabins of stone, logs or pine boards stood among the trees. Some of the cabins had names on markers beside their drives. All were tightly shuttered and untenanted. Snow was banked around them and lay heavily on their roofs.

He traveled about a mile and a half before the woods thinned out and he could see meadows beyond. He passed a high, wooden structure with a loading platform and a sign reading: "ICE HOUSE—LAUREL FLATS." A broad driveway turned into it, curving to come parallel to the loading ramp. Another drive branched from it to circle the building. The drives had been used recently.

Rather suddenly, he broke into cleared land and found himself in a broad, shallow valley, sparsely wooded with aspen and pine. There were more cabins dotting the landscape, accessible by narrow roads in a random network. Just ahead he saw a junction where a road turned off and ran in a straight line across the valley toward more woods a mile or so away. On a large marker at the junction were the words: "LAUREL FLATS," and below, over a long arrow pointing down the road to his left, "PEABODY HOTEL."

He saw the smoke first, a curling black column beyond a slight rise. As he drove toward the marker, very slowly now, the building came into view by degrees, vertically, like an approaching ship at sea. A high mansard roof, a row of dormer windows, then the square, blocklike façade of the old frame structure, from the top down, a row of high, narrow windows at each of three floors, ranked with geometric precision across the front and on the side that he could see from his angle on the through highway. Finally he could see the long porch across the front, a short, broad flight of steps descending to a drive that curved in a long, slow arc from the valley road. There was a stand of pine trees beyond the building. The road continued beyond the hotel, disappearing into more woodland.

Just short of the turn and marker, he stopped the car abruptly. A long, black Cadillac, with motor idling, sat on the hotel drive. He could see the pale puffs of the exhaust, slowly rhythmic. He put the car in reverse and backed straight down the road as far as the icehouse. From there, only the upward-drifting smoke from the hotel was visible. He glanced at the broad drive and it looked solid enough. He turned into it, drove fast toward the loading platform, then swerved to circle the building. The snow was soft on top but there was a hard crust underneath and it supported the light car.

He pulled in close to the rear wall of the building, where a loading chute and a row of oil drums formed a protected runway, largely clear of snow and invisible from the road. There were trees along the road between the icehouse and the corner where the valley road turned off to the hotel. He walked in ankle-deep snow, moving behind the trees, to the junction and looked down toward the hotel.

The car was still drawn up in front of the long porch. There were no others in sight. Mickey stood in the snow that drifted into his shoes, slowly soaking his feet, and waited. Five minutes passed. The front door of the hotel opened and a woman in a fur coat and shiny patent-leather boots came onto the porch. With her was a tall man in an overcoat and white scarf, carrying a suitcase. They stood for a few seconds on the porch, then moved down to the Cadillac. The one with the suitcase helped the woman into the front seat under the wheel, then put the suitcase on the back seat. He closed both doors and leaned into the front window for a moment, then stepped back. The car rolled slowly down the drive to the road. The woman put out a gloved hand and waved and the man in the overcoat waved in reply. Then he turned and went back up the steps and into the hotel.

Mickey walked back behind the trees toward the icehouse, watching the road, keeping out of sight. He got a look at the woman as the big car passed. She was around forty, he guessed, and good-looking in a severe way, with a straight nose, and a small, tight mouth. She looked neither right nor left as she drove.

Mickey got into his car and drove slowly toward the road, stopping short of it. He looked down toward the canyon, but the big car had wound out of sight, though he could still hear it. He waited till the last of the sound had died away, then turned into the road, turned again at the junction and drove to the Peabody Hotel. He parked on the drive and climbed the steps. There was a bell forged by a blacksmith from heavy iron bars, with another bar to strike it with. He rang, lightly at first, waited and rang again. He waited a couple of minutes and the door opened. The tall one, without the overcoat and scarf, looked out at him. He seemed startled, but no more than that. Mickey gave him a long chance to look him over. His own pulse was pounding in his temple like a powered hammer. His hands in his pockets opened and clenched tight.

Because it was him, all right. It was Lou Roberts.

10

He looked back at Mickey without recognition. He was neither friendly nor hostile, but seemed annoyed. Mickey waited for him to speak.

What he finally said was, "Yeah?"

"I need a room for the night," Mickey said.

"A room—look, it's practically Christmas."

"You mean you're closed?"

"Yeah—this time of year? Well, not exactly closed, but nobody comes up here in the winter."

"Well, I happened to come up to look over some property, and I figure it will be late before I start back. So I don't feel like driving down that canyon after dark and they told me down below I could put up at your place."

Roberts frowned past him, then shouldered the door open reluctantly.

"We've got the room, I guess, if you don't mind the service. I'm all alone for a couple of days."

"All I need is a bed," Mickey said.

He walked into a large entrance hall, high-ceilinged, with a handsome staircase winding up to the second floor. Beyond the staircase was a hall leading to the rear of the building. There was a waist-high counter in one corner with a bank of open mail slots behind it. A sign carved in polished wood read: "PEABODY HOTEL—ELIZ. PEABODY, PROP."

Roberts led the way to the desk, where he went behind the counter and shuffled through some odds and ends as if he didn't know what to do with them. There was a small desk set with a pen and clips to hold registration cards, but there were no cards in place.

"Not my end of the business," Roberts grumbled. "I don't know where in hell she keeps the stuff."

Mickey took out his wallet.

"What's the rate?" he said.

Roberts shrugged impatiently.

"I don't know. Single rates in the summer are ten dollars a day."

Mickey tossed a ten-dollar bill on the counter.

"It's worth it to me not to have to drive down tonight," he said. "Nobody knows I'm here. Forget the red tape."

Roberts dropped the bill into a drawer.

"You got any luggage?" he said.

"One bag," Mickey said. "I can handle it."

He walked outside. He got his suitcase out of the back of the car and when he got to the porch with it, Roberts opened the door for him.

"It'll have to be a room at the back," he said, turning to the stairs. "We can't keep the whole place heated all winter."

"Sure," Mickey said.

He carried his own bag, following Roberts up the winding stair. There were intersecting halls on the second floor, with rooms along the outside wall from front to back and on both sides of the transverse hall, front and rear. Roberts led him toward the back to the fourth room down the hall. When he opened the door, a draught of cold air swirled around them.

Roberts went in ahead and, stooping, turned on a large steam radiator. It hissed and banged metallically. Mickey set his bag on a luggage rack in front of a high window. The shade was drawn and when he raised it, he looked out over the valley to the near mountains, high and snow-covered. The scattered pines in the valley were filled with snow and among them he could see cabins, half buried. The road that ran past the hotel continued for some distance and he lost sight of it among the trees. On the slopes rising from the valley he saw more of the old mine shafts such as he had noticed in the canyon.

"It'll take a while to warm up," Roberts said. "You better wait downstairs. About time for lunch."

"All right," Mickey said.

Roberts was wearing a richly embroidered Western shirt, black slacks and loafer shoes. He stood slightly taller than Mickey, was well set up, with black, wavy hair and brown eyes.

A gigolo, Mickey thought. A real ladies' man.

He took off his gloves, pushed them into his coat pocket, took off the overcoat and laid it over his suitcase. Roberts looked at him with some curiosity as they left the room, but no trace of recognition showed in his eyes.

"I didn't know there was any property for sale up here," he said, as they went downstairs.

"The owner didn't want it spread around," Mickey said, "until we could make a deal. I told him I'd just look around."

On either side of the lobby, glass-paneled double doors opened into adjoining rooms. To the left at the foot of the stairs, Mickey saw a small shop stocked with fishing tackle and souvenirs. Beyond the store was a barbershop with a single chair.

On the right, the doors gave onto a small tavern and cocktail lounge. Roberts led him in there.

"I don't know how good you'll eat," he said, "but the bar's open twenty-four hours a day."

It was a warm, comfortable room. Above the small back bar was an antique harness yoke and a mounted elk's head. There were some large leather armchairs and a leather sofa with a curving back rest. There were a few tables with casual chairs. The bar featured a brass rail; there were no stools. The lounge occupied the front corner of the building, and toward the rear another set of doors opened onto a dining room. In the dim light, Mickey saw bare tables with chairs stacked on top of them.

There was a fireplace in the lounge and Roberts picked a log from a well-stocked woodbox and tossed it onto a bed of slow-flickering coals. A fountain of sparks filled the firebox momentarily and the wood crackled and snapped, igniting.

Roberts offered a drink and Mickey declined. He sat down in one of the armchairs, facing the fire, and propped his wet feet on the hearth. He watched Roberts pour a generous slug of whisky into a squat, thick glass.

"Miss Peabody isn't here?" Mickey said.

"She had to go to Denver for a couple of days," Roberts said. "She's got folks there."

Mickey shifted his feet on the hearth. He could feel his shoes stiffening as they dried.

"How old a woman is Miss Peabody?" he said.

Roberts was pouring himself another slug.

"She's not too old," he said.

Mickey waited for him to expand on the reply, but nothing more came. He wasn't discouraged. It would come. It would all come, even the worst of it....

They sat over steak sandwiches, potato chips and whisky in the tavern. Mickey wasn't hungry, but the meat was edible and he chewed on it doggedly, now and then taking a sip of the whisky. From time to time he was aware of Roberts studying him.

"Funny time of the year to look at property up here," Roberts said.

"It was the only time I could get away before spring."

"What business you in?" Roberts asked.

"I travel."

"Spend any time in Denver on the way up?" Roberts asked.

"A couple of weeks. I had business there."

"Money business, or monkey business?"

"Some of both."

Roberts chuckled with approval.

"If you're going back that way," he said, "I can give

you some numbers."

"Okay," Mickey said.

They finished the meal and Mickey helped carry the dishes back to the kitchen through the vast, cold dining room. In the lounge again, they sat by the fire and Roberts drank some more.

"Denver's not bad," he said reflectively, "but, man, that Kansas City. That's the greatest."

"You spent time there?" Mickey said.

"Yeah. There are girls in Kansas City—anything. Anything you want, you know? People talk about Las Vegas. Hell, it's nothing."

"You spent time in Las Vegas too?"

"Long time. Too long."

That's where he got that suntan, Mickey thought, and probably those Western clothes, too.

"Don't you get lonesome up here, with no girls?" Mickey asked.

"When that time comes, I'll move," Roberts said. "It's not exactly no girls. There's Liz."

"Oh," Mickey said. "I forgot."

It was about two o'clock. Mickey stretched and got up and looked out the front window. The weather hadn't changed since before lunch. It was gray, cold, but quiet.

"I don't know anything up here," he said. "You feel up to showing me around some?"

"Outside?"

"Just up the road a ways. I'll pay a guide's rates. Don't want to be out long."

Roberts shifted his long form indolently.

"I guess I got enough whisky in me to stand it for a

while," he said. "Better get your coat. From now on, it won't get any warmer out there."

From the porch, Roberts, in a heavy leather jacket, ear muffs and boots, looked dubiously at Mickey's small car.

"Better take the Jeep," he said. "You can run yours in the garage."

"All right," Mickey said.

A drive ran along the east side of the hotel to a large building at the rear. Roberts walked back to open the doors, while Mickey got the small car started and drove it into the garage. The interior was spacious, but much of it was taken up with stored furniture and household effects. There was an empty slot where the Cadillac had been parked and against the wall stood a Jeep, its top removed.

It took a few minutes to get it started and warmed up. Mickey waited outside till it backed out, then closed the big doors and climbed in beside Roberts. They turned slowly onto the drive, the Jeep protesting but making it all right when they hit soft snow.

"Which way?" Roberts shouted, as they reached the road.

Mickey pointed west, toward the woodland. Roberts shrugged, put the Jeep in gear and turned in that direction. The road had been scraped recently, but lay under several inches of snow. Where the crust had softened, the heavy Jeep broke through and the ride was rough.

They passed cabins on both sides of the road. All were deserted, their windows sealed with heavy shutters.

"Nobody up here at all?" Mickey said.

"Nearest person," Roberts shouted, "is four miles up the road."

The road dipped entering the woods and the snow was deeply drifted. The Jeep sank in to the tops of the wheels, slid, lunged and came out of it, grinding. On the level again, they wound for half a mile through a miniature forest of pine and aspen, with cabins set far back in clearings.

They came out on a shallow slope strewn with snowcapped boulders and a few stunted pines. Ahead, he could see how the road began to climb sharply into the mountains. At the far edge of the slope, the road forked. One branch wound off along a ledge of rock toward the north; the left fork continued roughly straight ahead. Roberts, with a kind of dogged hospitality, pushed the Jeep hard through the ruts to the fork.

"Only place to turn around," he said.

He swung onto the right branch and stopped. Roberts waved his arm.

"That's about it," he said. "You find the property you're interested in?"

"I think so," Mickey said. "I don't know if I'm interested."

In the triangle formed by the road fork was one of the old mine shafts, a square, timbered entrance into an outcropping of rock. Snow was banked shallowly at the entrance. A broken, narrow-gauge railroad track emerged from it. A rusted ore car sat on the track. Miscellaneous debris was scattered here and there.

"Isn't it kind of dangerous for kids, with those old mines?" Mickey asked.

"I don't know," Roberts said. "I never fooled around in them."

He reached behind the seat and brought up a heavy-duty flashlight about a foot long.

"You want to take a look," he said, "go ahead. I'll wait."

Mickey took the flashlight, climbed down and walked up to the mine tunnel, staying clear of the ore car as he passed. He had to stoop slightly to enter. As soon as he passed the outer portal, it was dark. He switched on the light and saw that a half-rotted timber had fallen at one end and partially blocked the entrance. Debris was scattered over the floor. A segment of the railway had been broken and lay in twisted fragments. He could see that the shaft ran level for some distance, then dropped off. Timbers were laid vertically at intervals against the rough rock walls and anchored to crossbeams overhead. The air in the shaft was damp, with an odor of rusted metal and rotting wood.

As he approached the drop-off, he saw it was the result of a cave-in. The tracks continued beyond a ragged hole some ten feet across. He walked to the edge cautiously and threw the light beam downward. The hole was maybe fifteen feet deep. Timbers and pieces of twisted track had fallen into it, along with other debris. He picked up a rock and dropped it into the hole. It banged dully on a timber and came to rest. He looked at it for a minute, then turned and made his way out of the shaft. Despite the grayness of the day, he found himself blinking against the sudden whiteness of the surrounding

Roberts was waiting for him in the Jeep. He gunned the motor suggestively as Mickey approached. Mickey put the flashlight away behind the seat and climbed up.

"Very interesting," he said. "Never saw one of those before."

Roberts backed the Jeep carefully along the ledge and into other branch of the fork.

"Lot of guys put a lot of sweat in those holes," he grunted, "and for nuthin'."

"That's the way it goes," Mickey said.

He pushed back his overcoat sleeve and looked at his watch. He found himself pressing hard with both feet against the floorboards of the Jeep.

11

They put the Jeep away and closed the garage. Roberts didn't bother to lock it. In the lobby, Mickey said he thought he would go up to his room and change his wet shoes, take a rest.

He opened his suitcase and took out a pair of dry socks; set his shoes on the radiator to dry. He draped his overcoat over a stiff-backed leather chair and sat down. After a while he got up, unlatched his door and left it barely ajar. Then he returned to the chair and sat with his hands on his thighs, waiting.

Gradually the room darkened. He had looked at his watch once, at three-thirty. The next time he looked it was a quarter to five and he could hear Roberts coming upstairs. The footsteps reached the top of the staircase, hesitated, then went on briefly. Mickey heard a door open toward the front of the hall.

He waited another half hour. From time to time he could hear the sounds Roberts made in the room down the hall. At five-fifteen, the door opened down there and he heard Roberts go down the stairs. He sat waiting for another five minutes. The room was dark now and he could see a thread of dull light along the edge of the doorjamb, light coming from downstairs. Then he heard music, a hi-fi record player, booming loud for a few moments until the volume was adjusted and it faded to a steady, distant rumble.

Mickey wiped his palms carefully on his trousers, got up and looked into the hall. The light came from the lobby. The music was down there, too. Even with the volume at a reasonable level, it would make a good covering sound.

He left the room and walked down the hall. Nothing sounded underfoot. No board creaked. It was a well-seasoned building and in the damp weather the joints had swollen tight.

Roberts' room was much like his own, but with less furniture—masculine and plain, almost Spartan. The bed was badly made, but there was no litter or disorder. He searched it, working quickly but silently, his movements efficient and economical. Half a dozen suits hung in a closet and he checked all of them thoroughly, turning the pockets out, feeling the fabric between both hands to make sure nothing had been slipped under a lining. He knew that when two people team up to commit a premeditated crime, each is likely to retain some concrete evidence implicating the other, as insurance against betrayal. This was what he hoped to find.

He found no such evidence in Roberts' clothing, nor in his luggage, stored on a high shelf in the closet. Nor in the chiffonier in one corner. In one of the shallow top drawers of the chest he found a mellowed leather case containing a set of six razors. They were in good condition. He opened them and saw that the blades had been honed recently. The steel was bright and clean and well cared for.

In another drawer he found a small package of photographs of various women. Most of them were nudes—nearly all of them on the bizarre side. Irene was not among them.

He was approaching the large four-poster bed when the music stopped suddenly. He hesitated by reflex, then went on, keeping his eye on the door. It wouldn't matter much now if he were discovered. It would be inconvenient, not according to plan, but in the long run, it wouldn't make much difference. He took his time searching the bed.

There was nothing to be found in it and at length he gave up. It was disappointing to find nothing, but he would get the information in other ways. He took a last look to make sure he had covered everything. The music had resumed downstairs. He could feel the vibration of the thudding beat. He left the room and went down the long staircase, across the lobby and into the bar.

Roberts was stretched out on the old leather sofa, a

drink in one hand. He had changed to a white shirt with long, full sleeves and an open collar, and had put on the loafer sandals again. There was a bottle of whisky on the bar. Mickey got a glass and poured half a shot into it. He stood with one foot on the brass rail. The fire was burning briskly, casting a rosy-yellow glow over the old, polished wood.

After a while he said, "We were talking about girls."

Roberts shifted on the sofa and chuckled in his throat. Mickey's hand squeezed tight around his glass.

"I was just thinking about that," Roberts said. "Remind me to give you those numbers in Denver."

"Maybe I ran into some of them when I was there," Mickey said.

"You'd know if you had."

"I would? How would I know, if they didn't tell me?"

"Well, between you and me, since you're just passing through here, I got a way of leaving my mark on a girl. Like a brand, you know?"

Mickey took a sip of whisky, swallowing with difficulty. His throat felt parched. His heartbeat had stepped up and he could feel it in his temples and just under his Adam's apple. Roberts had begun to spill sooner than he had hoped. But it wasn't too surprising. Men like Roberts could barely refrain from bragging about their conquests.

"How do you do that?" Mickey asked.

Roberts' hand slid inside his shirt; reappeared. Like a miniature lightning flash, the long blade of a razor flicked into view.

"I'm a barber by trade," he said. "That's how I came up here in the first place. Liz advertised for a barber."

Mickey drank a little more whisky.

"You mean you cut these girls—with a razor? How do you get away with that?"

Roberts chuckled. Mickey's foot was cramped in his stiff shoe, as if his toes were trying to curl over the rail.

"You have to know how to handle the blade," Roberts was saying. "You don't want it too messy."

He slashed delicately, swiftly, at the air.

"Like that—once, twice, three times—it's done. She's had it. And she always remembers."

Mickey brushed at his eyes with the back of his hand.

"I guess she would," he said.

"Now you're with it," Roberts said. "She surely would. Now you're getting the picture."

Mickey ran his hand out along the curved edge of the bar and pulled it back slowly.

"I've got the picture," he said quietly, "now that you mention it. Somebody did that to my wife."

"Your wife!"

Roberts stiffened on the couch, the razor in mid-air. Then he sank back, shrugging.

"Well, it wasn't me," he said.

Mickey drank what remained of the whisky. He set the glass down carefully, pushed it away with his fingers.

"Yeah," he said. "It was you."

Roberts went stiff again. He pushed himself up on one elbow. The razor, open, lay along his thigh.

"You're nuts, man," he said.

Mickey jerked his head impatiently. He had both

feet flat the floor. He could feel the hard edge of the bar across the middle of his back.

"It was you, Lou Roberts," he said, intoning it in a dry, monotone. "Five and a half months ago, in a house in the country not far from Chicago; it was you and one other, with my wife staked out on the floor, and she died of it."

Roberts sat up on the couch. His head shook strangely, incompletely.

"Oh, no," he said softly. "No, you got the wrong guy. I was never—"

There was a sudden shot-like report in the fireplace and Roberts jumped.

"It was you," Mickey said. "I was there. You let me watch."

"No," Roberts said. "Oh no—"

Mickey stood against the bar, waiting. Roberts came slowly to his feet, his eyes rigid.

"It couldn't be," he said. His voice rose. "He shot you! Killed you!"

"No," Mickey said. "Nobody killed me."

For perhaps thirty seconds, Roberts, in an awkward, strained crouch, stared across the room. Then the razor flashed in the firelight and he came on, rushing.

Mickey waited till it was too late for the other to change the direction of his lunge, then sidestepped, pivoting. The razor slashed down past his shoulder, struck the bar, and Roberts slammed his ribs against the edge. Mickey's fist smashed at the back of his head and Roberts gasped and let go of the razor. He turned, groping, and Mickey hit him hard in the ribs and with his left in the side of the jaw. Roberts' head snapped to one side and he careened backward across the room, falling short of the sofa. He started up, shaking his head. Mickey waited, gauging his swing. Aiming carefully, deliberately, he struck Roberts full force on the bridge of his nose.

Roberts screamed and collapsed against the sofa. His mouth and chin blossomed like rare, red fruit. Mickey walked to the hi-fi set in the corner and turned it off.

He kicked one of the chairs into position, facing Roberts, sat down on it and waited. After a couple of minutes Roberts roused and wiped his mouth with the white sleeve of his shirt. He put one hand on the sofa, started to get up, then gave in and stayed where he was.

"What're you going to do?" he said. "What do you want?"

Mickey looked at him in surprise.

"What do I want?"

"I mean—" Roberts shouted shrilly. "What do you want?"

Mickey leaned forward on the chair.

"Who was the other one?" he said.

Roberts stared, shook his head.

"You got to give me a chance," he said. "I'm entitled to a fair trial. You can't—"

Mickey nodded, looked at his hands.

"I'll give you a chance," he said. "I'll let you fight me for a fair trial. Right now."

He went behind the bar and found the razor Roberts had dropped. He brought it back, folding the bright blade into the handle. With a flip of his wrist he tossed it to Roberts. It fell on the floor. Roberts groped for it, found it, released the blade. Mickey watched him stiffen, gather himself, working up to his knees against the sofa. Then his arm reached out over it and began with measured, compulsive strokes, to cut long slashes in the smooth, aged leather.

Mickey lunged from the chair, caught Roberts' shoulder and jerked him around. The razor slashed at him feebly and he used his forearm against the other's wrist.

"Don't give me that phony psycho crap! Talk to me, Roberts!"

Roberts snuffled in his broken nose. With slow, mechanical strokes he stropped the razor blade on the taut fabric covering his thigh. Then without warning he slashed upward at Mickey's throat. Only half prepared, Mickey threw himself backward and to one side, tumbling into the clear toward the bar. He heard feet pounding heavily, going away. When he found him, Roberts was plunging into the lobby.

He was halfway up the stairs when Mickey reached him. The taller man half turned, cutting down at Mickey's face. Mickey twisted, gripped the banister with both hands and kicked Roberts' feet out from under him. Roberts fell awkwardly, rolled down the steps. He had sense enough to let go of the razor as he fell. Momentarily stunned, he lay in a still, cramped heap at the bottom of the staircase.

Mickey picked up the razor and put it in his pocket. He lifted Roberts at the shoulders and dragged him into the bar, propped him against the sofa. He slapped his face lightly, alternately with the palm and back of his hand till Roberts came around, blinking. Mickey crouched, facing him.

"Now you talk to me," he said quietly. "The sooner you start, the easier it will be. Because I can make it hard for you, Roberts—the way you did for her—Kathy."

Roberts' eyes rolled to one side, then the other.

"I'll refresh your memory," Mickey said. "On the floor, remember? All staked out, helpless, a gag in her mouth—she couldn't even scream. I can fix it for you to have the same deal. I don't think it would take long."

Roberts pressed back against the sofa, panting. His mouth moved soundlessly.

"Who was the other one?" Mickey said.

Roberts mouthed something, tried again and made it. "Frenchy," he gasped. "Guy named Frenchy Wister."

"All right," Mickey said, "we got a start. Where does Frenchy Wister live?"

"California—"

"Where in California?"

"In—down south, like in the desert—"

"Where?"

"Yuma—near Yuma, Arizona."

"You said California."

Roberts' throat convulsed violently.

"It's between Yuma and—El Centro. There's a big hotel—resort—"

"Frenchy Wister's resort?"

"No. He owns a motel—"

"What's the name of the town?"

"Vista del Sol."

"Why do they call him Frenchy? Is he French?"

"No. I don't know."

"Where did you meet him?"

"In Vegas—Las Vegas."

Mickey waited till Roberts' eyes met his.

"Which one of you had the idea? About Kathy?"

"Him—Frenchy—honest to God! It was him!"

"You just went along?"

"Yeah—that's right."

"What for? Kicks?"

Roberts shook his head vigorously.

"No—for money."

"How much?"

"Five hundred—and expenses."

"Five hundred dollars."

It wasn't a question; simply a low-voiced, unbelieving murmur. Mickey got up on stiff legs and made his way to the bar. He poured some whisky into the glass and drank it. When he looked around, Roberts was as he had left him, on the floor, cowering against the sofa. Mickey rubbed his face roughly with both hands.

"Why?" he said.

"I don't know. Jesus, I don't know! It was something Frenchy had to do."

"Why did he have to?"

"I don't know."

"How did you know where to go? How did you find Kathy?"

"Frenchy had a name—and a town."

"What name?"

"Phillips—Mickey Phillips."

Mickey started toward him. Roberts snuffled and

edged away along the sofa.

"I'm Mickey Phillips," Mickey said. He stabbed at his chest with his thumb, shouting. "Me! I am Mickey Phillips!"

Roberts ran his tongue over his lips. Mickey halted himself, sucked air deeply into his lungs and sat on the chair, facing Roberts.

"All right," he said. "Tell me what you did. The part I didn't see."

"Nothing—we were finished—"

"Tell me what you did! Everything."

We—the woman was—dead. Frenchy took out a gun. He—shot you—"

"Then what?"

"Then—he told me to take the handcuffs off you—because they could be traced, he said. He looked around—for stuff that could be tied in—"

"What else? Go ahead, what else!"

"He—he took a picture—"

"He *what?*"

"With a flash camera—he took a picture—"

"Of who?"

"Of—her—the woman—"

"Why? Why did he take a picture?"

"To prove it—to prove we did the job—"

Mickey lunged at him. Roberts turned and tried to scramble on to the sofa. Mickey grabbed his shirt collar. The collar ripped away and the shirt opened down the back.

"Prove it to who?" Mickey shouted. "Who was he doing it for?"

"I don't know."

Mickey grabbed Roberts' hair and pulled his head back, twisting.

"Who hired Frenchy to do it?"

Roberts shook his head helplessly and wiped at his face with a ragged sleeve. Mickey went to the bar, started to pour a drink, then changed his mind.

"Listen," he said, speaking calmly again, "you better work on this, Roberts. We're up here all alone and I've got nothing to lose. Nothing."

Roberts rubbed his face with his arm. Mickey sat down on a chair and waited. Except for Roberts' snuffling and the tired crackling of the dying fire, there was no sound.

Ten minutes passed. The long, unnerving silence prodded Roberts and he shifted against the sofa.

"What—more do you want?" he said.

"Who hired Frenchy Wister to cut up somebody named Mickey Phillips?"

"I don't know."

"Work on it!"

"Honest to God—I don't know! I tried to find out. He wouldn't tell me."

"Did you know it was a woman he was after?"

"No, not at first."

"When did you find out?"

"Just before—that day—before we did it."

"What did Frenchy tell you?"

"He just told me—what to do."

"Tell me."

Roberts' throat worked. Pushing up, he got on his feet and moved unsteadily to the bar. Mickey let him pour a good-sized shot and drink it. Roberts coughed and wiped his nose gingerly with his arm.

"Go ahead," Mickey said.

"We were staying in this—place—outside of Chicago. He told me to stay there till he got back. It was in the morning. He left and I hung around. He didn't get back till—I don't know—late in the afternoon. 'Okay,' he said, 'let's go.' I asked where we were going and he said just down the road a ways."

Roberts poured another drink.

"So we drove about an hour and a half, through some towns, mostly country. I kept asking him—where were we going, but he wouldn't tell me anything. We were practically there before he told me anything. Then he said, 'This broad lives down the road here. We're out in the country; shouldn't be any trouble. She's probably shacked up with some guy. So we knock on the door and whoever comes, you say, "Does Mickey Phillips live here?" If the answer is Yes, we go in fast. If it's a guy, hit him hard enough to keep him quiet.'

"So then I asked him, what if the answer is No? And he said, 'Then we go away. We got the wrong place.' And I asked him, if he wasn't sure this was the place, what the hell were we doing there? And he said, 'I'm sure it's the place, but the phone book was last year's.' So then I didn't ask any more questions."

Mickey was staring at him.

"He looked it up in the phone book?" he said. "He just looked it up?"

Roberts picked up the bottle. Mickey went to the bar, grabbed the bottle and smashed it in the fireplace. Roberts slid backwards along the bar, watching him.

"Where was Frenchy all that day while you were

waiting for him?"

"I don't know."

"That picture he took. You got a copy of it."

"No! I've got no copy—"

"You must have. You save pictures. I saw them upstairs in your room."

"Not that one. Honest to God I never had a copy. I never even saw it."

Mickey reached for him and Roberts stumbled backward, ducking.

"What did you do after? After you were—finished?" Mickey said.

"We just got in the car and started driving. The first night we drove to some place in Kansas City. The next night he dropped me off in Pueblo and I took a bus to Denver."

"Where did Frenchy go?"

"He said he was going back home."

"To Vista del Sol?"

"That's right. He owns a motel there."

"What's the name of it?"

"I don't know. He never told me."

"All he told you was when you were almost there and he said there was this woman who got herself in trouble."

"That's all."

"And that was enough for you, huh? That and five hundred dollars."

"What do you mean by that?"

"I mean—after you got inside. After you saw her— my wife—Kathy—did she look like a woman asking for that kind of a deal?"

"I don't know. I didn't—"

"They're all the same to you, huh?"

"No."

"When they're naked and you got a razor in your hand, it's all the same to you—"

"No! If I'd known who it was—"

"Shut up!"

Mickey's hand was sweating and it slipped on the smooth, rounded edge of the bar. He looked at Roberts' blood-smeared face and knew that the moment in which he could have killed him had passed. Maybe it had passed long before—that horrific night, when they had begged for killing and he had been tied up, helpless. He tried to recall it now, to push himself back in time to the horror of that night. But he couldn't remember. He felt panic. How could he forget? Roberts' face swam in his vision, and when he tried to replace it with the image of Kathy, he failed. It became Roberts and he saw there was nothing here to kill. Roberts was nothing, a blob, a breathing vegetable. In his life as a policeman, even the lowest, cheapest bum he had ever brought in had been an individual human being, a personality. Some had joked, some had cried, some had put up a fight. Roberts was nothing.

"This Frenchy," Mickey said. "Married?"

"He said so. A Mexican girl."

Mickey moved along the bar toward him and Roberts moved back, keeping step, rounding the return end of the bar, his hand trembling on the edge.

"Who do you care about, Roberts?" Mickey said. "Who means a lot to you?"

Roberts shook his head jerkily. He came to the dead

end of his retreat, against the wall beside the back-bar mirror. "Liz Peabody?" Mickey said. "You care about her? Big lover boy. You carved your initials on Liz Peabody yet?"

Roberts crouched against the wall, staring.

"No—no, I never— Look, what more do you want from me?"

"Not much," Mickey said.

"Listen, give me a break. I swear to God if I'd known who she was I never would have done it. He forced me into it. He conned me—"

"He conned you with five hundred dollars."

Roberts' legs gave way. He settled downward slowly till he was on his knees, one hand clutching at the bar. Mickey's voice was strange in his own ears, toneless and remote.

"I am placing you under arrest. I will take you to the nearest detention facility and charge you with the murder of Kathleen Phillips on the night of July two, this year. Get on your feet."

Roberts shook his head vaguely. Mickey bent, seized his belt and yanked upward.

"I said get up!"

Roberts came to his feet, hunched over, supporting himself with one hand on the edge of the bar. Mickey twisted and pushed him forward. Roberts stumbled, caught himself and walked to the center of the lobby, where he stopped.

"Upstairs," Mickey said behind him. "Get a coat."

Roberts looked half around.

"Liz—" he mumbled.

"Let's go," Mickey said. "You can get in touch with

Liz later. Maybe the sheriff will let you make a phone call."

It's going to be a long way to a sheriff, he was thinking. Then I got to hang around and go through the routine over it. And when that other one—Frenchy—when his name gets mentioned, there's a good chance he'll get tipped before they can pick him up. That must be close to the Mexican border where he lives in California. He may not even be there now, and the longer it takes to find him, the more chance he'll be tipped off. Maybe I ought to take Roberts out there with me, before I turn him in. That way I could maybe use him against the other one.

But Jesus, he thought, all the way to California!

"Come on!" he said sharply to Roberts. "Upstairs. I'm right behind you."

Roberts made it to the stairs, got hold of the banister and started up. Mickey gave him plenty of start.

Going up after him, he was thinking, These local people aren't going to like it, the way I'll bring him in, all roughed up. They're not going to believe me. They'll have to check back, while I sit around. If I could pin a note on him and dump him on the steps …

Eight, nine steps above him, Roberts had paused. Mickey paused with him, waiting, no longer impatient, trying now to think it out, do a little planning. He looked down over the banister at the hotel desk, with the telephone and pen set.

If I could call in, they could check the story while we were on our way. I wouldn't have to tell them I had Roberts—

Then he heard it, like a muffled thud, felt a subtle

change in air pressure. He glanced up in time to see Roberts hurtling down on him from above, literally flying through the air, his bloody face twisted. Mickey tried to flatten against the banister, gripped it with one hand, but Roberts' full weight struck him at that moment in the groin. He gasped for air and the impact tore his hand from the rail. He tumbled with Roberts, helpless and in agony, over and over, down the steps.

By a wrenching effort, he managed to hunch and draw in, to take the final fall on his back and shoulders rather than his head. He was fuzzy in his mind and, for a moment, helpless on the lobby floor, but he was conscious, and free of the weight of Roberts' body. When his vision cleared he saw the taller one scrambling upward, reaching. Mickey was on his knees when Roberts turned on the stairs and the razor flashed in his hand. He felt his empty pocket and knew that Roberts had retrieved the only weapon at hand.

Mickey's eyes fixed on the other's feet, which would first betray the moment and direction of an attack. He rose stiffly, forcing his knees to lock. The knifelike pain in his groin nearly brought him down again. He made himself back off slowly, his eyes wary on Roberts, who now had no more to lose than he. The pain dulled as he moved, and he steadied inside. After a moment he extended one hand, the fingers curled.

"Come on," he said. "You want to be that big a fool—I was hoping for this."

Roberts brushed at his eyes with his free hand and started down the steps. He held the razor well out to one side. He was invulnerable to attack, but he could be handled, Mickey knew, if he could be brought to make the first move.

They were eight feet apart when Roberts cleared the last step. Mickey waited with slack arms.

"Any time, Roberts," he said. "Or would it be easier if I put my hands in my pockets?"

The taunt was lost on Roberts. He advanced slowly, directly, giving no hint of a feint to either side. He was just short of arm's reach when he stopped. Mickey backed off two steps, forcing him to come on again. There was a fixed grin on Roberts' face, made hideous by the swollen nose and the smeared blood.

Mickey backed off again and Roberts hesitated, then came along. They moved in a series of rhythmic fits and starts, a macabre dance—two steps back, two steps forward, two steps back. Mickey felt his shoulders come up against the wall beside the heavy slab front door. This was going to be it now, any second, and what he had to remember was to keep his eye on the razor, no matter what, even if Roberts should feint with a kick to the groin, the deadly hand was his exclusive concern.

The kick came, sudden and vicious but short. Mickey's guts twisted with the effort, but he kept his eye on the weapon. It moved in a silver arc toward his throat, then veered downward. He hunched his left shoulder into it and slashed at Roberts' forearm with his own, felt the blade slide off his sleeve. Before Roberts could move inside to cut upward toward his face, he slammed his right fist into Roberts' belly. Roberts sagged and slashed at him wildly. Ducking, Mickey tripped and fell to one side, landing heavily

on the wood floor. Then Roberts was on him, gasping
for breath and for a couple of seconds Mickey lost
sight of the blade. He felt it rip at the side of his jacket
and a momentary sting under his left ribs. He got a
knee up into Roberts' belly, used both hands and
heaved him clear, then scrambled to his feet. They
were in the center of the lobby now. Still clutching the
razor, Roberts came up into a crouch, shaking his
head. When he charged Mickey was ready. He hit
Roberts with his left fist in the ribs and the razor cut
toward him feebly, then wobbled in mid-air. With his
right fist, and nearly all his weight behind it, he
smashed at the bloodstained face.

Roberts careened backward, his back arched, fought
for balance and, failing, stumbled against the newel
post at the foot of the stairs. The sound of his head
striking the solid wood was an ultimate, sudden-end
sound. He fell on his side across the lowest step, rolled
over once, then lay still.

Mickey found himself leaning against the desk, with
stiff hands, panting for breath. After a minute he went
to Roberts, looked at one of his eyes and felt for a
pulse. He couldn't feel any. Roberts appeared to be
dead; if not yet, then soon, very soon. Suddenly it was
cold in the lobby.

12

It seemed to him that a long time had passed before
he decided what to do. Actually it was no more than
eight or ten minutes, and the sum of his reasoning

came to this:

There's no way to take him in now and keep those other two—Wister and the one who hired the two of them—from finding out about Roberts and lamming out. The local law here would hold me till they check clear back home, and maybe more than that. They would have to. By then they could never catch up with the others. There's no other way; I'll have to do it myself.

He looked at where Roberts lay sprawled on the step. Mickey was sure now he was dead.

One thing, he thought, nobody knows about it yet. Only me.

He climbed the stairs, went into Roberts' room, found a suitcase and packed as much into it as he could. He left a few things. It didn't have to be perfect. Roberts was a wastrel. Walking away on impulse, he might logically leave behind what it was inconvenient to carry.

When he had closed the suitcase he found a rag and moved about the room, wiping carefully everything he might have touched. It took him nearly an hour. He went to the room he had rented and got into his overcoat. He left the rest of his things and returned to the lobby. He set Roberts' suitcase near the front door, went outside and walked back to the garage. He was mildly surprised to find it was snowing. It snowed softly, silently, an undulating interruption of his vision against the night sky. He could feel it on his face and in his hair.

He found the key to the Jeep, got it started and warmed it up for five minutes. Then he backed out and swung around to the front drive. He went into the hotel and searched till he found the razor. He put it in his own pocket for safekeeping. He took the suitcase out to the Jeep and put it in the front seat. Then he went back for Roberts.

The body was heavier than he had anticipated. He got it onto his shoulder after some work and carried it outside and down to the Jeep. He dumped it into the back and made sure it wouldn't roll out, then returned to the porch and closed the front door, making sure it was unlocked.

He drove carefully in the direction of the brief tour they had taken earlier. It snowed continuously, but quietly, evenly. When he reached the dip in the woods, he saw that already the earlier ruts were barely discernible. The Jeep fought its way through the low spot and got onto higher ground. He drove in low gear to the fork in the road and swung as close as possible to the entrance to the abandoned mine. He parked facing it and left the headlights on, but when he started into the tunnel with the suitcase, he found the illumination extended no farther than half a dozen feet into the passage. He went back and got the flashlight, returned to the tunnel and carried the suitcase to the edge of the pit he had found earlier. He tossed the bag into the pit and watched dry dust spray up around it. When the dust settled, he went back to the Jeep and carefully worked Roberts' body onto his shoulder.

It wasn't like carrying the suitcase. The soft snow was deceitful underfoot. Twice he nearly fell. Inside the passage, he had to work his way over the fallen timber and nearly collapsed under his clumsy burden. By the time he reached the edge of the pit he was panting and his shoulder and back ached under the drag of the dead weight.

He stood looking down for a few seconds, then backed up two or three paces from the edge. There was too much weight casually to toss it away. He could feel himself falling in with it and being unable to get out. It would be a bad place to die. It was a bad place for Roberts to wind up, but Roberts had asked for it. It was too late to worry about that.

He knelt slowly and dumped the corpse onto the floor of the tunnel. It was a relief to get rid of the weight. He was shaking with tension and it took him a couple of minutes to get his breath and settle down. Then he got on his knees and rolled Roberts' body toward the edge. It hung momentarily on the point of dropping off. He gave it a strong push, heard it slide, then tumble dryly into the hole. He got to his feet and threw the flashlight beam into the pit. The body lay in an awkward sprawl twelve or fifteen feet below the level of the tunnel floor.

Deep enough, he decided. There was little chance anyone would enter this shaft during the winter. The external signs of his approach to it would be covered by the snow, probably by the next day. It wasn't cold enough in the tunnel to preserve the body intact. By spring it would be a skeleton.

He made his way back to the Jeep. He had started to back into the turn when he remembered the razor in his pocket. He climbed down, went back into the tunnel and tossed the razor into the pit. It landed on

Roberts' sprawled right thigh, poised precariously, then slid off to the ground. He went back once more to the Jeep and started the short drive to the hotel.

In the garage he checked the Jeep for signs of the use he had made of it. There were stains here and there and he cleaned them off, using an oiled rag he found on a nail. He wiped the steering wheel and all the places he might have touched the Jeep. He replaced the flashlight where it had been stowed, got into his own car and backed it out of the garage. There were tire marks where it had been, but they were overlapped by others and on the dusty floor would not be noticeable except under close scrutiny. Liz Peabody, he thought, might spend some time grieving for her lost lover, but he doubted that she would launch an investigation. He judged her to be a woman of some pride, though not much sense. Still she would probably have sense enough not to call in the local sheriff to find her boyfriend who, apparently, had run away.

He closed the garage, drove to the front drive and returned to the hotel. In the tavern, where the fire had died, there was surprisingly little muss. He decided there was nothing he could do about the slashes Roberts had made in the leather sofa. The same would go for the broken bottle in the fireplace. They were things Roberts might have done while drunk. There were bloodstains here and there and he cleaned them up as well as he could.

There was more to do in the lobby and he worked at it methodically and at length. When he finished, he looked at his watch and it was five o'clock in the morning. There would be only two more hours of darkness and it would take him at least an hour to drive down the canyon.

He went up to his room at the back of the building, turned off the radiators, drew down the shades and restored the room to the condition it had been in when he had come. He wiped off everything he had touched, put on the gloves he had removed hours before, picked up his suitcase and went out.

After he had got in the car, he took a last look at the high, square building. The snow was falling in thick, slow waves, without wind. Even as he watched, it piled grayly on the wide steps, covering his footprints, laying a soft film of obscurity over his path from one world to another. He put the car in gear, worked his way onto the road and drove off toward the canyon. The snow fell silently, filling the tracks of his departure.

He checked into a motel on the road to Denver and went to bed. It took him a long time to get to sleep and when he woke in the middle of the afternoon he felt stunned by fatigue. He made himself get up, drove to a public telephone booth and made a call to the Denver airport. Then he put in a call to the downtown hotel where he had left Irene. Her voice was drowsy when she came on, but quickened when she recognized him.

"Hi, honey, where are you?"

He couldn't tell whether she had anyone with her. He didn't care, except that if there was someone

listening it would be a bad time to mention Lou
Roberts.

"Still want to go to Las Vegas?" he said.

"Sure, honey."

"You can get a plane tonight at eight o'clock. Meet
me at the airport."

"Sure. Well, how will I get to the airport?"

"Just have a boy carry your suitcase down to the
lobby and call a taxi. The hotel owes you a refund on
advance rent. Stop at the desk and ask for it."

"Okay. But I haven't got a suitcase."

He braced himself against the wall of the booth and
forced himself to speak patiently and distinctly.

"You'd better buy one," he said. "The hotel owes you
at least forty dollars. You can get a good suitcase for
forty or fifty."

"Well—okay, Joe."

"Be sure to make it on time. I won't be able to wait
for another plane."

"Sure, honey. Where shall I meet you?"

"At the United Air Lines Terminal. Ask the taxi
driver when you get to the airport. He'll show you."

"All right. Be seeing you, honey."

When he hung up he was sweating lightly. The air
was an icy blast against his face as he left the booth.

He checked out of the motel, had lunch at a roadside
café and he got to the airport in time to pick up Irene's
ticket. It was six o'clock by then and there was no
sign of Irene. He bought a newspaper but found he
couldn't make himself read it. Only its date finally
seeped through to him. He realized it was two days

before Christmas. He toured the airport concessions in search of a gift, finally settled on a bottle of good whisky in a Christmas package.

Irene arrived at seven-thirty-five. He saw her pause in the entrance and search the room with her vague, defective vision. When she found him, she lifted her hand in tentative greeting. She was wearing her new coat and a new hat she had bought for herself. Her goods legs strode freely and she wasn't putting on much wriggle. When she reached him, a little breathless, smiling with those teeth, he caught her in one arm and kissed her, hardly realizing what he was about. It was a surprise to her, too, and she looked at him with some suspicion.

"Hello, Joe, did I make it?"

"You made it."

He helped get her luggage weighed in and they learned her flight had been delayed by forty-five minutes. He took her into the cocktail lounge and settled with her for what she had had to spend for the suitcase and taxi. When he gave her the Christmas bottle she showed embarrassment.

"Gee, thanks, honey—I didn't get you anything."

"I didn't want you to. Save your money. Do you know anybody in Las Vegas?"

"Well, there was a girl I knew in Kansas City. She went out there a couple of months ago."

He took two one-hundred-dollar bills from his wallet and handed them to her.

"This ought to take care of you for a couple of weeks," he said. "Do you like to gamble?"

She grinned, suddenly, frankly.

"I don't know," she said. "I never did."

"If you want some advice from an old man, don't get the habit."

"Some old man," she said. "Why don't you come with me?"

"I can't. Maybe I'll look you up someday."

"Did you see Lou Roberts?"

"No. I talked to him on the phone. He wasn't interested."

"Why don't you come to Las Vegas? You tired of me, Joe?"

"No, nothing like that."

"I know sometimes I'm bitchy. I'm sorry for when I was bitchy to you."

"Forget it. I gave you a bad time, too."

"No, Joe, you never did. And you could have, easy. Because I went for you. I still could."

"I'm glad you feel that way. I like you too."

He reached across the table and took her hand. Her eyes held on his for a moment, then fell away.

"Any time you change your mind," she said.

Then they were calling her flight and he helped her out of the booth. She was muttering nervously. Guiding her through the crowds up the ramp, he could feel her tension in the thrust of her flexed arm against his side. A big plane nearby was revving up and she stopped suddenly and put out one hand, as if for support.

"Joe—I never did this before. I was never on a plane."

He put an arm around her waist.

"You don't have to get on if you don't want to, but it's nothing to worry about. Like riding a bus."

She gazed at the swirl of passersby, ran her tongue over her lips and went along. There was time for him to see her aboard and he helped find her seat and make a disposition of her small effects. The flight was not sold out and she had a seat by the window and nobody in the aisle seat. He leaned over her, found the ends of her seat belt and showed her how to fasten it.

"Take care of yourself," he said.

"Okay, Joe."

He kissed her face quickly, taking leave. Her face changed suddenly. She seized the lapel of his coat, tugging, and he leaned down close.

"My God," she said, "I almost forgot—there was a guy looking for you. He came to the hotel."

He felt a sensation as of a large, cold hand squeezing his belly.

"What did he look like?" he asked.

"Kind of a nice guy—older than you."

"Did he ask for me by name?"

"Yeah. He had a picture of you."

"When was this?"

"The other day—yesterday I guess."

"What did you tell him?"

"I said you checked out and I didn't know where you were."

Her breath battered his face in quick, warm puffs.

"Was that all right?" she asked.

He patted her absently.

"That was fine."

The stewardess was making her way along the aisle and it was time to go. She lifted her face and he tried to kiss her cheek, but she moved her mouth to his and kissed him fully, frankly, without embarrassment.

"So long, Joe," she said. "Thanks for everything."

He waved goodbye and got off quickly. From the boarding ramp, he looked back. He found her window, but she wasn't looking his way. The stewardess was leaning over her, probably, he thought, showing her the seat belt. He lingered until the plane pivoted and began to taxi slowly toward the runway, then turned back to the terminal.

Carefully and over a long period of time, in the men's room, at the newsstand and other points and in the cocktail lounge, he tried to discover whether he was being followed and, if so, by whom. After an hour, he had discovered nothing. The constant shifting of the crowds at random made it impossible to pin down suspected shadows. He considered it over a drink.

Since leaving his hometown, he had made no friends, aside from Irene, who might try to look him up. Briefly he thought of the pimp Patsy whom he had mugged in the alley on behalf of Irene (and himself). But he hadn't done Patsy injury enough to send him on a cross-country manhunt.

One thing that hung him up was that the guy had shown Irene a picture. There had been no circulation of his picture at any time, that he knew of. He had been "mugged" for his police ID card, but more than five years before. He had destroyed that ID card after examining the mug shots in Chicago. Or had he? He felt certain he had destroyed it, but couldn't call up any associations connected with it, such as a hotel room, a lavatory, a city trash can.

Maybe it was not a thing to remember. In a way it was like tearing up the book of his own life—a thing to forget.

He abandoned the effort. The important thing was that Irene had warned him. Somebody was looking for him and had come within hours, maybe minutes, of stepping on his heels. Regardless of his identity, there was the chance that already somebody knew about the death of Lou Roberts. He thought it very unlikely that the shadow was Frenchy Wister. But there had been three of them in it—Roberts, Wister and a third, unknown, unrecognizable.

He finished the drink and went outside by way of the ticket office. Nobody followed or noted his passage, that he was aware of. He joined an outgoing lane of pedestrian traffic between the terminal and the parking lot. Within sight of his own car he stopped and took time to make sure nobody was waiting for him in the vicinity. Then he went on, unlocked the car and got in, locking the door again after he was seated. He turned on the overhead light and checked his suitcase. It had not been tampered with. He pulled out of the parking slot, worked into the lane of outgoing traffic and drove back toward the city.

He stayed with the main stream for some distance, then started an intricate maneuver of windings and switchbacks, working his way into quiet neighborhoods where a tail would be easily discernible. Eventually he found himself driving several blocks at a time without a sign of a car behind him and he began looking for a way back to the main highway. In a gas station he had the car serviced and asked for a road map and directions to the highway south toward Colorado Springs.

He drove for about three hours and stopped at a motel on the edge of a small town. He had selected it because during the last four miles of his approach he had seen nobody behind him and because it featured closed garages, where his car would be invisible from the road. He went to bed with a feeling of some security and slept undisturbed for six hours.

He was on the road again at daybreak and he stopped for breakfast near Trinidad. The day was cold and clear, and he made good time. He drove carefully, without pushing, and felt good about having shaken off the shadow, but refrained from congratulating himself. There was a long way to go and too much at stake to risk frustration. Still, he breathed a deep sigh of relief when he reached Highway 66 and turned west toward California.

13

The town called Vista del Sol was a sun-swept cluster of white-stucco and simulated-adobe buildings on both sides of the highway. To the south were rolling hills of sand that put him in mind of pictures he had seen of the Sahara. Dominating the landscape was a large, rambling structure of pink stucco on a low hill about a mile north of the village. The town was connected with it by a blacktop road winding between two rows of stunted palm trees. Driving out from Yuma he had seen signs directing travelers to the Montezuma Inn.

It was the day after Christmas and although the temperature, in the high sixties, was normal for that time of year, it wasn't what Mickey was used to. In Yuma that morning he had seen girls wearing shorts. Ropes of tinsel, with red-and-green wreaths suspended from them, stretched across the main street. As far as he could see, it was the only street in town, except for the road leading up to the inn. The buildings, all but two or three, appeared to have been built within the last eight or ten years. There was a uniformity of design about them, as if they had been conceived by one man for a single purpose.

Through a casual inquiry in a local café, he learned that Frenchy Wister was manager of the Yucca Tree Motel at the west end of town. It was an L-shaped, two-story structure, with a large swimming pool, surrounded by the defiantly green, stiff grass of an irrigated desert lawn. There was a large, odd-looking tree made of plywood, and a sign hanging from it read: "VACANCY."

The office was the first unit at the front, downstairs. He saw a bell on a small desk and rang it lightly. Beyond the desk, through an opening between drapes in a narrow doorway, he could see part of a room containing a sofa and some chairs. He was braced to confront Frenchy Wister as he had confronted Lou Roberts at the mountain hotel, to meet the issue of recognition or nonrecognition at once and get it settled. So he was unprepared when the door opened behind him and a young woman came in from outside.

"*Sí?* Yes, mister?" she said, coming to the desk.

She was a Mexican girl, very dark-skinned, of twenty

or twenty-one. She wore a white blouse with a red trim and a full peasant skirt, gaily colored. Her long black hair was tied with a red ribbon and hung straight down her back. Her eyes were smoky-dark, almost black, though the pupils actually were brown. Her features were regular and somewhat less refined than many he had seen along the way, but the bold modeling of her face gave her a stronger, more vigorous look. She had large breasts under the thin blouse and he could see by the way she moved, in spite of the full skirt, that she was lithe and young in body.

"You're the manager?" Mickey asked.

"No, *señor*. My 'usband. He is not here."

"I would like a single room."

"Yes. You sign here please?"

He signed the registration card she gave him, using the name Joe Marine. When he finished, she studied the card carefully, underscoring his name with a strong, work-worn finger.

"Mister—Mah-ree-nay?"

"Muh-reen," he said.

"Mah-reen. Okay. How long you want to stay?"

"I don't know. A few days."

"*Seis*—six dollar a day, Mister Marine."

He paid her for one day. She put the money in a drawer, picked a key from a rack and handed it to him. Stepping outside with him, she pointed along the paved veranda, formed by the overhang of the second story.

"*Nùmero* fourteen, *señor*," she said.

"Thank you," he said.

As he got into his car and started up the drive toward

the garage that adjoined his room, he saw her stride vigorously along the veranda to a cart piled with linens and cleaning implements. She was carrying the entire load of the establishment without help that he could see.

He opened his suitcase on the bed, hung up his spare suit and put the rest of his clothes away in a bureau designed in bleached maple to match the modern, low-slung bedstead. The room was clean and insidiously comfortable. He sat down on the bed and suddenly he was desperately tired and apprehensive about his undertaking.

It had been simple enough, even aside from the lucky and wholly unpredictable circumstances of location and isolation, once he had traced him, to get what he wanted from Roberts. But Frenchy Wister was another matter. If what Roberts had said was true—and all he had told him, with minor deviations, had checked out so far—Wister, too, had been a hired hand. Therefore, information would have to be wrung out of Wister, who might be tougher than Roberts. There was the difference, too, that Wister apparently had a wife. And there was the big difference that he would be dealing with Wister, not in a remote, deserted cul-de-sac, but in Wister's own community, where probably everybody knew what everybody else was doing most of the time, or ought to be doing.

But the new, unexpected fear in him he laid to the unknown shadow. For the first time he had to look behind as well as ahead. The greatest danger was that he might let himself be pushed. If he grew edgy, feeling time at his heels, he could blunder badly; and one blunder might be the total of his allotment because it would be intricate and hazardous. He would have to force himself to take time, develop a groundwork that wouldn't shift on him just when he had come to count on it. A direct approach to Wister could be self-defeating. He would have to be broken down, demoralized in advance.

He went to the window, opened the blinds with his fingers and looked out. The Mexican woman was still at work with her cleaning. There were two women lying by the pool in the sun. As he watched, they got up, gathered their things and moved toward the motel in his direction. The blond one, he thought, looked a little overgrown and flabby, but the dark one, much smaller, was in good shape. She had nice legs and a good bust—better than Irene's, as he remembered. He watched them turn into a room three doors from his own. The blonde entered first and the brunette glanced toward his room for a moment before she disappeared.

He watched the Mexican woman trundle the cart along the veranda, her long, gay skirt swishing from side to side with the action of her sturdy hips.

One of the most effective ways to demoralize a man, as he knew too well, was to destroy his home. But before he could attack Wister's home, he would have to find out what "home" involved for him. The Montezuma Inn appeared to be the nerve center of the village and was likely to be the main source of information.

He locked the door of his room, knowing it was a

haphazard precaution in a commercial building. He lay down on the bed fully dressed. Within five minutes he was asleep and when he woke, the sun had gone down and it was dark in the room.

He got up, took a shower, shaved and dressed in his better suit. He was surprised at the sharp cold when he stepped outside, but decided not to return for his overcoat. He walked along the veranda toward the office. There were no lights in the room occupied by the two women from the pool. He went on to the office and inside. A dim light burned on the desk. He could smell food cooking in another room. He waited a minute, then rang the bell.

The drapes in the doorway billowed gently and the Mexican girl appeared between them. She was wearing a loose, unbelted wrapper that she held together with one hand over her breasts. Her feet were bare.

"Yes, *señor*—Mister Mah-reen?"

"I'm sorry to bother you," he said. "I was wondering about a place to eat."

She lifted her arm wearily, pointing.

"Is a little place downtown, pretty good. Only other place is the inn."

She blinked slowly, shifted her feet and settled her body carefully, as if to make sure she could stand. He lingered, watching her, and she remained, waiting stoically. When she blinked again, her eyes failed to open immediately and she swayed.

"You're very tired," he said. "I'm sorry."

He moved past the desk toward her and she showed neither shyness nor welcome.

"I am all right, *señor*," she said. "I think you like the inn okay." (She pronounced it *Een*.) "Very good food."

He touched her arm gently. She drew away.

"You ought not to work so hard," he said. "Don't you have any help?"

"In season," she said. "Need no 'elp now."

"When your husband is here, does he help?"

"Need no 'elp, Mr. Marine."

"How long will he be gone—this time?"

She closed her eyes, put her head back and he thought for a moment she was going to fall. Then she shook her head briskly.

"*Tres, cuatro* days," she said. "I will be all right, *señor, gracias*."

He gazed at her till she returned his look.

"Tell you what," he said, "why don't you have dinner with me?"

"Me, *señor?*" she said, her face coming alive with surprise. "No—mus' stay here. People come."

"We won't be gone long. You need a good meal, a little time off."

She retreated in stoical silence, shook her head firmly. "No. *Gracias*. Mus' stay."

He hadn't expected her to accept his invitation, had only wanted to plant an idea. Studying her impassive brown face, he couldn't tell whether he had succeeded.

"Maybe tomorrow," he said, smiling.

As he moved to go out, somewhere in the building a door slammed suddenly. He saw her start violently and the quick flutter of a pulse in her throat. It told him something, but he didn't get the message until later.

"Good night," he said, and he went out quickly.

There were no more than half a dozen people being served in the dining room at the Montezuma Inn. It was a large room and the scattered diners appeared isolated and remote from one another. A small, worried-looking man wearing glasses and a tuxedo scurried to greet him and led him to a table. Mickey ordered a highball and the little man snapped his fingers imperiously and dashed off.

The design and decor of the resort owed something to the Aztecs, but not much. Pseudo primitive figurines adorned the walls and a few niches, and above a giant fireplace was a brass disk symbolizing the sun. But the carpeting and furniture and the expanse of plate glass in the outside wall were strictly modern U.S.A. Outside the window, hidden spotlights threw into relief jagged rock formations, a desert landscape. In the foreground was a large swimming pool with cabanas at one end. Facing it on three sides were detached cottages, designed to match the main building. Beyond, toward the rear, other cottages flanked a wide, curving drive.

Not far from his table sat the two women he had seen at the motel swimming pool. Twice during his meal he caught the brunette's eye and she returned his glance without expression. One more customer, a middle-aged man with severe arthritis, came slowly into the dining room and was seated. The others, who had finished, went out singly or in pairs.

The waiter was bringing his coffee when a large, rotund man came in from the lobby, paused a moment to speak to the worried headwaiter, then came on to shake hands with the arthritic gentleman. He was a big man. Mickey estimated his height at six feet six and his weight at close to three hundred pounds. But he was broad and big-boned and the weight was evenly spread. He had a round face and wore horn-rimmed glasses. There were a few strands of light-brown hair brushed across his nearly bald scalp. His manner was hearty when he greeted the guest, but after he had pulled out a chair and sat down, his voice fell to a low pitch.

Only one other incident occurred that seemed worth noting. He caught sight of the undersized maître d' in violent controversy with one of the waiters. The waiter, an older man with gray hair and sagging shoulders, finally shrugged and walked away. The maître d' was distressed. Mickey finished his coffee, waited a while for his check and left the table.

He spent the rest of the evening in the bar, which was doing a business consistent with that in the dining room. It was a warm, comfortable room, with large booths around the walls and a small dance floor, not in use. Except for a middle-aged couple in one of the booths, he, the bartender and the two women from the motel had it to themselves.

By the simple means of buying a few drinks for the small house, he learned some elementary facts. The nervous maître d' was named Homer Bridges, and he was the active manager of the resort. The big man with the round face was Fred Teller, the owner. He learned that Mig, the brunette, was a schoolteacher from Los Angeles, that she supported an invalid mother, that she and Sandra, her companion, regularly spent their vacations together and that they had selected Vista del Sol this year because Mig couldn't afford Las Vegas.

After a couple of hours of conversation that had grown more and more forced, she startled him by asking outright, "Joe, are you married?"

"No," he said.

She seemed to give it some thought.

"I believe you," she said then, "because it's the day after Christmas and if you were married, you wouldn't be alone."

He supposed that was as accurate a way to figure it as any, though it took a few things for granted.

The girls left at midnight. The couple in the booth had gone long since and he shared the room with Charley, the bartender. Charley was dapper, sardonic and, Mickey had noticed, talkative, though he hadn't had much chance in the earlier part of the evening.

"Staying here at the inn?" he asked Mickey.

"No, the motel."

"Oh. Wister's place."

Charley, polishing glasses, shook his head in wonder. "There's a guy that's got it made, I tell you true. Got that motel, right on the highway, and a strong young Mexican girl to take care of it. He don't lift a *finger*, man! She takes care of the place and he goes to Vegas."

Pretty soon he said, "He must have won that motel in a crap game. I hear he was nothing but a bum till he started hanging around the inn here, running errands for Teller."

"Maybe Mr. Teller gave it to him," Mickey said. "I heard downtown that Teller owns everything around here."

Charley thought it over, shook his head.

"Nah, he never did anything that big for Teller. He's a flunky, you know? A messenger boy."

He worked on the glasses mechanically, not having to look when he picked them up and set them down.

"I'd like to know where he found that Mexican kid. I never saw a woman work like that."

"Maybe around Yuma—"

"Huh-uh! He got her across the border. She's a wetback if I ever saw one."

"Wetback?"

"Illegal immigrant. No papers."

"Don't they round them up, send 'em back?"

Charley shrugged.

"Who's going to strain? Sure, if there's a gang of 'em and they're drifting around. But one here, one there— I guess they might get Wister's girl someday but what the hell, he can get another one."

When Mickey finished his drink he bought one for Charley and himself. They drank together in silence until a carload of tourists in slacks and sport shirts came in and Charley got busy. Mickey waited a while, but the conversation never got back to Wister. At one o'clock he said good night, left the inn and drove back to the motel.

It was dark and quiet. If any new patrons had arrived in his absence, there was no sign of them. He went to his room, undressed and got into bed. He was tired and restless and found himself woolgathering. He felt he had goofed off, had spent money and engaged in frivolous conversation to no purpose. He felt guilty and, in flight from the guilt, he forced his mind back to the main stream of his mission. In the process, he remembered the quivering, naked fear in Wister's young wife when he had seen her in the office just before dinner.

After a while he got up and dressed in the dark. He stood at the window for some time, thinking, and then he left the room and walked along the veranda to the office-apartment at the front of the building.

There was no response to his ring. He waited in the cold swirl of the desert wind. When he looked at his watch, he saw it was after two-thirty. He hesitated a moment, then rapped sharply, staccato on the door. At length her voice came from the other side, close and hesitant, as if she had been standing there for some time trying to muster the courage to open it.

"Who it it?"

"It's me," he said. "Joe Marine."

He heard tumblers click in a heavy-duty lock. A chain grated and banged against the panel. A dead bolt slid back and she opened the door far enough to peer out at him.

"Yes, Mr. Marine?" she said. "Something is wrong?"

"May I come in?" he said.

Reluctantly she stepped back and let him in. She was wearing the same shapeless robe he had seen earlier and she held it tight at her throat, gazing at him with eyes dulled by weariness.

"Something is wrong, Mr. Marine?"

"Nothing wrong. I came to stay here with you so won't be afraid."

She gaped at him.

"With me—*señor*—"

"Not what you think," he said quickly. "I could see you were frightened to be alone. I'm not sleepy and I might as well sit around here as somewhere else."

"No, I am all right, Mr. Marine. You—"

He smiled steadily, feeling it as an unaccustomed stiffness in his face.

"You run along to bed," he said. "I'll just sit out here at the desk while you sleep."

Her eyes looked out of a primitive pool of suspicion and fear.

"Mr. Marine," she said slowly, "what you want? You not from the poleecy?"

"No, I'm not from the police and I'm not going to steal anything. You go ahead now, get some rest. You need it."

She continued to gaze at him with a mixture of puzzlement and suspicion. And then, either because she truly welcomed his presence, or because she was too tired to argue, she turned with a small shrug and walked out of the room. A moment later her face reappeared between the curtains.

"Mr. Marine," she said, "you like to sit in here? More easy."

"Thank you," he said, and followed her into the cramped living room of the apartment.

It was in precise order and immaculate. The furniture was inexpensive, blocklike, without color or excitement of design. But there was no dust, clutter or disorder. It was as clean, he thought, as a barracks just before inspection and it gave him that kind of feeling. Through an open door he saw an equally spotless kitchen.

She was looking at him with dogged patience and he guessed she expected him to sit down. He obliged, selecting a broad armchair. She waited till he was seated, then turned away into the bedroom. Even the slump of weariness failed to conceal the youthful grace and resilience of her strong body. He revised his earlier estimate of her age downward. It was possible she wasn't yet twenty.

She closed the bedroom door from inside, but a moment later she opened it and left it ajar. The rose-shaded lamp beside bed a double bed went out and he could hear the whisper of sound she made slipping out of the robe, and the quiet lurch of the bed as she got into it. He settled back in the chair and sat quietly, leaving the floor lamp burning beside it so that if she were watching, as he felt certain she was, he would not appear as a threat in her home.

A large heater at one side of the room gave off warmth and a faint odor of burning gas. It had no lulling effect on him, nor, evidently, on her. He could hear by her frequent turnings in the bed that she was unable to sleep. After half an hour he concluded that his intrusion had been a mistake, or anyway, ill-timed. None of his purpose could be served without her confidence. He decided to give it up for that night.

As it happened, his exit, with a pause at the bedroom

door to let her know he was leaving, coincided with a momentary stillness in the bedroom.

"I'm afraid I'm disturbing you," he said. "Do you want me to go now?"

There was an interminable stillness and he was about to go on and let himself out when he heard her speak from the dark recess of her bed.

"No—Señor Marine—you stay? *Por favor?*"

It took him a minute to decide whether she meant him to go or to stay. In the end, he translated *"por favor"* with literal roughness as, "do me the favor."

"Sure," he said. "If you like."

He started back to the chair, then swerved and went into the bedroom, slowly, so as not to alarm her. He could see her dimly, a small bulk buried to the chin in the big bed. He made out the black cups of her eyes watching him. He pulled up a straight chair beside the bed and sat down.

"You ought to sleep," he said.

"*Sí*—Mr. Marine—"

"My name is Joe."

After a pause, she said,

"Okay—Joe."

"Shall I turn out the light?" he asked.

"*Sí*, okay. You stay now—Joe?"

"Yes, I'll stay."

He went to the other room, turned off the lamp and returned to sit beside the bed. She had turned over and he could see the lush billow of her long black hair on the pale bedspread. She was still restless. From time to time she made a sound in her throat, as if in pain. He laid his hand gently on the spread, where it dipped to the small of her back. He felt her go tense at the touch but she made no protest. He began to stroke and massage her back slowly and firmly. Through the bedclothes he could feel the taut, serviceable sweep of her loins from the ribs to hips. Even after the cramped muscles had begun to relax, the young firmness remained.

All that woman, he found himself thinking, in a rhythm set by the stroking movement of his hand, all that woman …

Her passage from wakefulness to sleep was subtle as the dropping of a leaf, but he could feel it. Later he confirmed it by the softly regular rise and fall of her ribs and the new sound of her breathing. He left his hand at rest on her back for a while. When he lifted it, she stirred briefly but went on sleeping.

He returned quietly to the chair in the living room. He sat in the dark, hearing the low hiss of the gas heater and the occasional rumble of a passing truck on the highway. It had been part of his plan to make a systematic search of the apartment while she slept, but he sat where he was, remembering her with his hand, and eventually he fell asleep.

When he woke, she was coming from the bedroom, barefooted, wearing the colorful skirt of the day before and a fresh blouse. She had tied a ribbon in her hair and it swept down her back in a long ponytail. When their eyes met, she showed no surprise and he guessed she had got over that before he wakened.

"You like coffee, Señor Marine?" she said.

"That would be good," he said. "Thanks."

He waited in the big chair while she made the coffee. She brought it to him in a plastic cup and handed him a paper napkin. He drank it gratefully while she sat watching.

Neither of them made any reference to the night. But as he was leaving, after he had paid her another day's rent and in her strained, businesslike way she had put the money away, he glanced back and she was watching him. After a moment she lowered her eyes.

"*Gracias*—Joe," she said.

He nodded.

"What is your name?" he asked.

She hesitated, and then, with a rising inflection, as if asking his approval, "Margarita?"

"That's a beautiful name," he said. "Margarita."

He didn't see her again until midafternoon. He slept for a couple of hours and went down to the village for lunch. When he got back to the motel, Margarita was at her cleaning in the room next to his. Her back was turned to him as he started past the room and he decided to keep going and not risk startling her by speaking to her back. Then he saw that she was struggling with a heavy mattress, trying to turn it over on a double bed. Besides going at it the wrong way from a leverage standpoint, she was grappling with something too bulky for one person to handle. As he paused, looking in, she slipped and fell on one knee beside the bed. It was a slab floor and he winced, feeling the impact with her. The mattress flopped back, awry on the bed, and she knelt where she was with her face in her folded arms, panting. He walked in silently.

"Margarita?"

She looked up at him, her long black hair tumbled about her face. He stepped around her, where she sat in the nest of her skirt, and straightened the mattress on the bed. She got up and he showed her a trick, using the weight of the mattress against its bulk and they turned it. She was limping slightly and turned her back to him to raise her skirt and inspect her bruised knee. Then she brushed her hair back from her face and as he started out she said,

"*Gracias—muchas gracias.*"

He scratched his head, frowning, and said, "*Por— nada?*"

She stared at him.

"Okay?" he said.

"Okay, Joe."

For the first time since he had known her, she was smiling.

14

He went to the inn at nine o'clock and it was the same as on the night before, only drearier. He concluded that the brunette Mig was available as a pickup, and in a clinical way, testing his own powers, he gave some time to developing the possibility. But he gave up finally out of boredom with her chatter. When, after repeated hints from Sandra, she agreed to go home, he didn't try to detain her.

He learned nothing new from Charley and sometime after midnight he left and returned to the motel. Margarita led him through the same ritual of the tightly locked door, except that she opened it more readily and without preliminary questioning through the panel. Few words passed between them. She got into bed and he sat with her, as before, until she fell asleep.

He had no feeling of wonder at himself. He had grown so adaptable to day-to-day changes that sitting here through the night with the weary, frightened Mexican girl seemed almost routine. He found himself resenting the certainty that Wister would return to interrupt it. He wished he knew when it would happen and whether by day or night. He would like not to be asleep in the chair at the time.

There were other things he wanted to know about Wister, too, and he decided he had better get to it. He had maybe two more nights in which to go over the apartment and it would take time, with Margarita likely to wake up at any moment. It was of the most vital importance to him to win her trust.

He made sure she was sleeping soundly and closed the bedroom door. On a constant alert for a sound from her, he made a systematic search of the living room. It didn't take long, even though he was thorough enough to move heavy furniture and roll back the rug, section by section, until he was satisfied nothing was hidden under it.

The prime object of his search was the photograph Roberts had told him Wister had taken. He thought Wister would probably have kept it. If he had been hired to do the job, as Roberts had said, he would surely retain concrete evidence of performance, for his own protection, not to mention the blackmail potential.

Searching the kitchen was a longer job than the other, though not as bad as he had anticipated. There were few possessions to be removed from cupboards and drawers and replaced. But the strain of working silently, especially among dishes and pots and pans, left his nerves frayed and his hands shaking.

In the office, he went through the desk drawers carefully. He found where she kept the receipts, in a cigar box. It contained the money she had taken in, each payment clipped to the registration card for the room she had rented. A simple, efficient system, he thought. They could trust her with the money because she had nowhere to go and because Wister had put the fear of God into her.

When he looked at his watch, it was after four o'clock. His eyes were sandy with tension and lack of sleep. He put his head down on the desk and was asleep within seconds. He woke after a few minutes and returned to the living room. He slept in the big chair until Margarita roused him, coming from the bedroom.

"*Buenos días, señor*—Joe," she said. "I fix *café*—okay?"

"Okay wonderful," he said.

He watched her drowsily as she went about it. The short time he had spent with her had produced its effect. Two nights of sleep without fear had given her new vigor. His throat tightened at the lithe, vigorous play of her body, bending and stretching.

They had the coffee at the kitchen table and watched the slow sunrise over the desert. The slowly strengthening light gave her flesh the texture of burnished copper. They were for the most part silent. As he was leaving he explained that had to drive into town that day but would be back before night.

"Okay, Joe," she said gravely.

He had breakfast in the village and stopped at a service station, where he picked up a road map. His destination was the county seat. It turned out to be a two-hour drive and he got there shortly before noon. He found the courthouse and made his way to the Recorder's office, where at length he was handed a volume of recorded deeds to property in the vicinity of the Montezuma Inn. He spent nearly an hour with the records and came up with the following notes:

The Yucca Tree Motel was owned in joint tenancy by Fred Teller and Arnold Wister. Previously it had been owned solely by Fred Teller and, previous to that, in joint tenancy by Fred Teller and Mrs. Michelline P. Teller. The transfer from the joint tenancy of Mr. and Mrs. Teller to Fred Teller, sole owner, had taken place something less than a year earlier. The joint tenancy of Fred Teller and Arnold Wister had begun six months later. More specifically, it had begun ten days after Kathy Phillips' murder.

The Montezuma Inn was held in joint tenancy by Fred Teller and Mrs. Michelline P. Teller. There had been no change in the recorded ownership for more than three years. It had passed to the Tellers from the Imperial Investment Company, Inc.

He scanned the records on other properties in Vista del Sol, but found nothing of interest, except that much of the village was owned solely by Fred Teller, having passed from joint tenancy of Fred Teller and Mrs. Michelline P. Teller at the same time the motel ownership had changed. He didn't find the name Arnold Wister on any property except the Yucca Tree.

He returned the volume to the clerk at the desk, left the courthouse and found a place to have lunch. After he left the restaurant he stopped at a newsstand and, on an impulse, bought a paperback book called *Conversational Spanish*.

He was approaching the motel from the west when he caught sight of Margarita trudging along the highway toward the village. She had changed from her skirt to a pair of blue jeans and a sweater and had tied a scarf over her head. She carried an empty paper shopping bag that tossed in the afternoon breeze.

When he pulled up beside her and stopped, she looked at the car furtively, poised as if to run. Not till he opened the door on her side did she appear to recognize him. After a moment she got into the car and sat stiffly against the door on her side while he drove toward the village.

"It's a long walk to the market," he said.

She didn't understand the word.

"A—store—*tienda?*" he said.

"*Sí, tienda. Carnicería.*"

A truck bore down from behind, swerved out and passed with a grinding roar. He ducked his head, pretending alarm. She smiled a little.

"*Chiquito*," she said.

"*Chiquito?*"

She laid her hand on the dashboard.

"*Chiquito automóvil*—little—"

"Oh, *sí*. Little car. But *bueno. Muchos* miles, *chiquito* gas."

"*Sí*," she said.

The sunset had turned the distant hills to rose-gold. The harsh contours of the desert were softened by the fading light. He glanced out past her.

"Beautiful," he said. "*Que es—el* desert?"

She looked out and waved her hand vaguely.

"*El postre*. Desert. In Mexico *mucho postre*."

"*Sí*," he said.

He drove to the market in the center of the town and let her out in the parking lot. He stayed in the car, waiting. He didn't want to risk making her shy by overattentiveness. It grew dark and when she came out, after pausing a moment in the lighted doorway, she started straight across the lot toward the street. He called to her and she turned toward the car. He realized she hadn't expected him to wait for her.

"You wait for me?" she said as she got in with the half-filled shopping bag.

"*Sí*," he said. "I wait."

"*Gracias*," she said.

"*Nada*."

When he let her out at the motel she lingered a moment as if she would say something to him, but finally she only said "*Gracias*" and turned away.

He had no appetite for dinner and stayed in his

room until after eight o'clock. Off and on he studied
the Spanish book, but it was hard to concentrate. He
kept going over the notes he had made at the
courthouse. Carefully he refrained from jumping to
conclusions. He would have to know more and with
some luck, he could get Charley to open up again. But
there was no point in going to the inn early and
spending a lot of money for nothing. The quiet time in
the bar usually started after ten o'clock. It might be
different tonight, if the tourists he had seen in the
village were an indication of more business for the
inn.

Several times he had tossed the book aside and
stepped onto the veranda, on the point of going to the
office. But there had been some new arrivals and he
knew she was busy. By nine-thirty, the place had
quieted and he went down there. He told her he had
to go out for a while and she nodded.

"I'll come back," he said.

"*Sí,*" she said after a moment. "Okay, Joe"

He couldn't tell by her face how much stock she put
in his promise.

He got to the inn a little before ten and went into
the bar. There was more business than usual and
Charley had little time for him at first. He saw no
sign of Mig and Sandra. Homer Bridges, the frantic
manager, was in and out periodically and Fred Teller
came in twice to look around. Mickey caught himself
studying the man and had to force himself to look
elsewhere.

By eleven o'clock, most of the trade had left the bar

and Charley was cleaning up at a leisurely pace, carrying on a grumbling monotone as he worked.

"Run this nowhere joint like it was the Springs or somewhere. Big deal. Must cost Teller a thousand bucks a day just to keep it open. A sure thing none off it gets to me."

"Maybe business will pick up after the holidays," Mickey said.

Charley shrugged.

"I guess it's all the same to Teller," he said. "He'll be out from under any day now."

"Oh?"

"There was once a Mrs. Teller," Charley said after a glance around. "Divorce, a year ago. She gets the whole place as soon as it's final. She gave him a break—a year to wind up his affairs."

"How did she manage the settlement?"

"I guess she had some of her own dough in it. And, they tell me, she helped put it together. Come to think of it, she ran it. What they say, it ran great then. She had a talent for it. I never met her."

Charley looked around carefully and moved closer, dropping his voice to a confidential level.

"Besides, I guess Teller asked for it. He's a mean bastard. He's got that big jolly-boy front—your genial host and all that jazz—but he is a tough son of a bitch. I heard about some of his deals. And I been in a couple of beefs with him myself. I lost. Let's face it, I'm scared of him. I guess his wife was too. I hear he belted her sometimes, like to killed her."

He put away some glasses, nodded toward the empty dining room.

"Maybe you noticed how jumpy everybody is—especially Bridges, the manager. This chick is due to come back and take over and they figure Teller won't give up without fight. If you want to know, I figure the same thing."

"If she's got a legal claim," Mickey said, "how can he fight?"

"With Teller," Charley said, "he'll find a way. And I tell you true, I hope it's on my day off."

Some people came in to one of the booths and Charley left the bar to wait on them. While he was away, Teller came in. He stood at the end of the bar and nodded to Mickey, smiling with his big round face. Mickey said "Hello." Charley came back and after he had served the order and returned again, he stood for a while in murmured conversation with Teller. Mickey realized that at least part of the time, they were talking about him. Finally Teller went away. Charley came back along the bar, looking harassed, put his foot up on the sink and leaned on his knee.

"You been up to Vegas lately?" he asked out of nowhere.

"Las Vegas? Never have been there," Mickey said.

"Oh. Don't like to gamble?"

"Sometimes maybe, a little."

"Poker player?"

"I don't know if you could say that."

"Well, I mean you know the rules."

"Look," Mickey said, "what are you trying to tell me?"

Charley threw up his hands.

"The things I'm supposed to do for that son— Like

this— Mr. Teller was wondering if you'd like a friendly little game. There are three, four guys get together every so often in Teller's office—"

"Oh," Mickey said, "and you're supposed to see if I'm safe."

"Yeah. A couple of these guys are deputies with the Sheriff's office and they got to watch out for their own undercover men."

Mickey nodded.

"It's no clip deal," Charley hastened to add. "Just a friendly game. Teller don't want your money."

Mickey kept quiet.

"Anyway," Charley said, "Teller would like you to drop by the office if you got nothing else to do."

"Okay, Charley."

He finished his drink slowly and got down, leaving a good tip. Charley told him how to find the office.

On the way, Mickey pondered the invitation—or summons. It could be that Teller simply wanted another poker hand. Or he might want to get a line on an unattached guy with nothing to do but sit around and spend money.

Teller's office was plain and comfortable, softly lighted except for a bright, white fluorescent lamp on the desk. The only unusual feature was the man himself, who made the ordinary man-sized desk at which he sat look like a toy. His round face was cherubic with good will. He held out a hand in greeting.

"Nice of you to drop in, Mr.—Marine, is it? Sit down, have a cigar."

Mickey sat down but declined the cigar.

"Charley tell you what this is about?"

"He said something about a card game."

"Right. We have a friendly game every so often, three or, four of the local boys. Thought you might like to join us."

"Well, Mr. Teller—"

Teller raised his hand, chuckling.

"Be natural for you to suspect us," he said. "Have no fear. Furnish your own cards, if you like. We could use another hand tonight. Simple as that."

"I take your word for it," Mickey said. "What I was going to say was, it would depend on the stakes."

Teller brushed the thought aside.

"We're all working people around here. It's a friendly game—five-and-ten limit."

Mickey looked at him through the bright light. "Five-and-ten cents, Mr. Teller?"

The happy round face contorted as Teller fought to control it. It would have been funny if Mickey had been in a laughing mood.

"Well—" Teller cleared his throat—"possibly some other time."

Mickey got up. The telephone rang and Teller lifted a hand to detain him while he picked up the instrument.

"No hard feelings, Mr. Marine—one moment, please don't go."

Mickey waited.

"Hello, Teller speaking," the big man said. "Yes, this is Fred Teller. Speak up, please." His huge face leaning into the lamplight was rigid in concentration. "Where?" he said. "Yes, I've got it.... Yes, I'll send instructions.

Quite a shock, of course. Thank you for calling."

He hung up.

"Well," he said, "there'll be no game tonight, Mr. Marine. One moment, if you'll bear with me—"

He lifted the phone and asked for "Harry's room." The operator said something and Teller barked impatiently, "Wake him up! I want to talk to him."

After a moment, someone came on.

"Harry," Teller said, "we'll go down to the motel first thing in the morning. Don't be late."

He hung up, took out a handkerchief and dabbed briefly at his forehead.

"Sorry about the interruption, Mr. Marine," he said. "Very disturbing news. A close friend, business associate, killed in a highway accident—Nevada." He peered up from behind the horn-rimmed glasses. "Frenchy Wister," he said. "Guess you haven't met him yet—been away—Las Vegas—"

There was an almost total silence while Teller waited for him to say something and Mickey fought for words.

"No," he managed to say finally, "I never met Mr. Wister. I'm sorry. Good night and thanks for the invitation."

He started out, his legs wooden.

"Not at all, Mr. Marine," Teller said. "Hope you enjoy your stay with us."

15

By the time he reached the motel, his mind had settled into a working groove.

There was a speculative case against Teller, but he had no real evidence. All he had was the knowledge that Teller and Wister had been thick and that Wister had come into a share of the motel shortly after Kathy's murder. The rest was shreds of hotel gossip about Teller's divorce, his ex-wife, her plan to return. If the hard part of the gossip—Teller's meanness and tough dealing—was true, he could guess the Teller might try to prevent his wife's returning by any means at hand; especially if it meant sole possession of the inn. But this was nothing that could be wrung from Teller, as he had wrung information out of Roberts.

The motel was dark, except for a dim light between the blind slats on the door of the office. He put the car away, went into his room and washed his hands and face. He sat on the bed for a while, but he was restless and ridden by anxiety. If he wanted to salvage any possibility of completing the hunt, he would have to make a search of Wister's effects before Teller and Harry came around in the morning.

He went down to the office. When he tried the knob, he found the door unlocked. He went in and Margarita was sitting behind the desk, staring at him with eyes like cinders.

"I thought you'd be in bed by now," he said.

"You say you come," she said.

"You were waiting for me?"

Her eyes fell.

"*Sí*," she said. "I wait."

When he moved to her and put his hand on her arm, she rose quickly and stood quietly near him.

"Margarita—"

"*Sí*—Joe?"

"Nothing," he said. "You better get to bed now."

"Okay, Joe."

He locked the door with every device available, while she watched. He followed her into the living room, where she hesitated, looking back from the bedroom door. He nodded, smiling.

"*Hasta la vista*," he said.

She returned the smile experimentally.

"*Mañana*," she said.

She closed the door and he paced the floor of the small room. As she had said nothing about it, he assumed she didn't know about Wister's accident. He recalled that Teller hadn't bothered to explain to Harry the reason for his midnight call. Margarita would have to be told and he couldn't decide how to go about it. He had cast himself in a certain role for her and he didn't want anything to change it.

Role was the wrong word, he realized then. At the start, yes, he had set out to win her confidence by using confidence techniques. But the pretense had gone out of it in a hurry. He was unable to explain why she had taken such complete possession of him so quickly, but he accepted the fact.

The bedroom door opened slowly. It was dark in the room and after a moment of silence he heard her get into bed. He moved to the doorway.

"Feel good?" he said, "*Bueno?*"

"*Sí*," she said, "*muy bueno.*"

He went in and drew the chair up beside the bed. He sat with his arms on his thighs and looked at her face in the great black nest of her hair. She had the bedclothes drawn up, but with one arm out, her hand on her breast. He reached for it and she let him take it in both of his.

Pretty soon she said, "Joe, w'y you do this? W'y you come—stay here with me?"

"I don't know."

He lifted her hand to his mouth and kissed it.

"Yes," he said, "I know."

She withdrew her hand slowly and replaced it on her breast. There was a long silence and he thought she had fallen asleep, but she spoke unexpectedly, her voice so low he could barely hear.

"Joe—Señor Wister—not my 'usband."

"Oh," he said quietly.

"He tell me to say so, *porque*—poleecy. He give me paper to show, but is not so. For poleecy only."

"I see," he said, "*comprendo.*"

"In Mexico, people very poor. I try to find—work? *Trabajo*. No *trabajo*. Señor Wister say come with him, he pay me to work, nice clean place to live—I come."

He waited. Pretty soon she said, "Señor Wister very bad *hombre*, I think."

"Was he bad to you, Margarita?"

"*Sí*. Sometime I would run away, but—no money— poleecy—"

He took her hand again.

"You don't have to run away now," he said. "Señor Wister is not coming back."

She lay very still, watching him. "No come back?" she said.

"He had an accident, in a car. He was killed."

"He is dead?"

"*Sí.*"

When she said nothing more, he was nonplused. Finally he opened his mouth to say the first thing that might come to mind, but she spoke ahead of him, lifting her hand and raising herself in the bed.

"Joe—you go now? *Por favor?*"

"Go—?"

It shocked him. He had done nothing that called for her throwing him out. Then he realized she was only asking him to leave the room.

"All right," he said. "You sleep now, okay?"

"Okay, Joe," she said. "I sleep."

He went out and sat uneasily on the edge of the big armchair, waiting. He heard her get up and move about in the bedroom. He listened carefully a long time and did not hear her get back in bed. He began tensely to speculate. It could be, he thought, that Wister had instructed her to destroy certain things if anything should happen to him. She might carry out the order simply because she was used to following orders; or he might have frightened her with stories of what the "poleecy" would do to her if she failed to destroy them. He pictured the evidence he needed going up in smoke or being flushed down the toilet. Half a dozen times he got up and went to the bedroom door, then returned to the chair. He stuck it out for half an hour. There was an interval of a few minutes in which he could hear no sound. He hoped she had gone back to bed, then saw that now light showed under the door. He went over there and knocked sharply.

"*Sí?*" she said.

"May I come in?"

He opened the door and looked in. She was fully dressed, to shoes and ankle socks. She was wearing a heavy, shapeless overcoat, such as might have been found in a relief package, and had drawn a scarf over her head and tied it under her chin. At her feet was a bundle, made from one of her skirts, bulging, shapeless as the coat. Her face was a taut, pale oval as she returned his look. He moved his hands.

"Where are you going?"

"I go now," she said. "No more *trabajo*—poleecy come—mus' go. Mexico."

"But—you have no money. How will you get there?"

"Is okay," she said. "I walk."

She stooped, hoisted the bundle and slung it over her shoulder. It was like something he was seeing in another existence, as if there were two separate worlds, alien to each other but concurrent, and he was living in both at once.

The bundle on her shoulder had disarranged her scarf and she pushed it back, spilling her hair thickly around her face. She was slightly out of breath and he could see the quick rise and fall of her breasts, even under the heavy coat. She looked at him with black eyes, her lips parted, and he was face to face with what he had known without really admitting it.

He loved her. Not as he had loved Kathy. Not as he might have loved the brunette bar companion, Mig, for an hour, overnight, a week. Not with the odd, refracted affection he had finally come to feel for Irene, but as a man, seeing it, loves a hill, a tree, the shape of a country, as a place to live.

"Margarita—"

He took the bundle from her and dropped it, used his hands gently, urging her back.

"Sit down, please—*por favor*."

She sat on the edge of the bed and he pulled the chair close and sat facing her. His fingers loosened the knot of the scarf under her chin.

"Listen," he said, "I don't want you to go."

"Mus' go now, Joe—"

"I want you to stay with me. I will take care of you."

"You—? W'y, Joe?"

It was such a simple, direct question.

"Tomorrow," he said, "we'll go to Yuma, find a nice place to live; small, easy place. No more *trabajo*."

She looked at him as at a child, trying to make him understand.

"Cannot stay here, Joe. Poleecy come, put me in big truck—back to Mexico—"

"Listen, please," he said, putting his hand over her mouth. "I have some work to do—at the inn. It won't take long. We'll live in Yuma for a while. When I finish the work, we'll go to Mexico. We'll get married. Then we can go anywhere we want to."

He saw the confusion in her face. He was a little confused himself. He hadn't planned this. He had got started and it had come spilling out.

"Joe, w'at you say? Work—the inn—Mexico—*esposa? Mi esposa?*"

"*Sí*, whatever that means," he said. "Come on now, take off your things and go to bed. We can talk about it in the morning. *Mañana*. That's a great word—*mañana*."

He unbuttoned the coat and slid it off her shoulders. She was wearing one of the plain white blouses and a tight wool skirt. She sat submissive, her hands quiet on her lap.

"You'll stay, won't you?" he said. "I'll take good care of you."

She gazed at him a long time, then bent her head slightly. "*Sí*," she said. "Okay, Joe. W'en we go?"

"Tomorrow," he said.

He took her face in his hands and made her look at him.

Her mouth moved and he kissed her, lightly at first, then harder, deeper. She was stiff and unresponsive at first, then her lips moved and she put her arms around his neck. There was a spicy fragrance about her mouth, and the kiss, as she gave herself to it, went deep. He could feel it in her and the thrust in himself. He got to his feet, still holding her face and the shift of his weight forced her back on the bed. Her knees rose as she fell. He was strongly aroused now. He pushed the skirt back on her thighs and she was naked under it. "Joe—" she said, "no—*por favor*—"

"Margarita—"

She seized his arms, pushing at them.

"No, Joe, not here! Not this place. *Mañana*—"

"Because of Wister?"

She looked away.

"*Sí*," she said. "Was bad here. Always bad."

His rage passed as quickly as it had come. He smoothed her skirt down, covering her, sat on the bed and lifted her into his arms.

"I'm sorry," he said. "Not here, not tonight."

She clung to him, her face hot against his.

"*Mañana*," she whispered. "Okay, Joe—*mañana?*"

"*Sí*," he said. "*Mañana.*"

She held onto him tightly for a long time and then her arms relaxed and fell away and she crouched, Indian fashion, her eyes brooding at him in the half-dark. Suddenly she roused, crawled past him and off the bed and went to a built-in wardrobe on the far side of the room. Below it, a shallow drawer extended from wall to wall. He watched as she tugged it open and reached into it, digging under a pile of stored blankets. Belatedly he moved to help her, then stopped as she brought out a metal strongbox, black, the size of a large cigar box. She set it on the floor, returned to the wardrobe and searched among a row of men's suits hanging at one end. When she came back, to kneel over the box, she had a thin key in her hand. The pulse in his temples throbbed dully.

She had some trouble with the lock.

"Señor Wister—very bad *hombre*," she said, her breath short.

She made the key work, raised the lid of the box and rummaged among a few papers. Finally she found what she wanted, lifted it up to him with both hands, a macabre offering. With a glance that twisted his stomach into a tight knot, he saw the thing he had been looking for. It was a snapshot-size photograph of the torso only. The face didn't show, nor the legs below mid-thigh.

He took it from her carefully, fighting to keep his hand from shaking.

"Señor Wister show me this—" she said, gazing up at him. "W'y, Joe? W'y?"

He made himself look at it, as if he had never seen it before, and then he slid it into his jacket pocket and reached to help her up. She swayed against him.

"I don't know why," he said, leading her to the bed. "But you won't have to look at it again."

He made her sit down on the bed. He kissed her gently, then went to the box, closed and locked it and put it back in the drawer under the blankets. He put the key in his pocket. Going out, he paused at the bed and put his hand on Margarita's face. She touched it with her own, then began, casual and heedless, to unbutton her blouse.

"Sleep now," he said. "I'll stay."

"Okay, Joe. I sleep."

He sat down in the big chair and after a while began to examine his priceless evidence. After the first shock, he found he could look at it with some objectivity. He couldn't see how it would be useful to anybody except as a morbid memento. The body was not identifiable. If he hadn't seen the horror with his own eyes, he doubted that he himself would know it to be Kathy. How could it serve any purpose as evidence of a mission accomplished? Surely the victim would be known to whoever had hired Wister to do it.

Or maybe he only knew a name. But why Kathy? Or, for that matter, why Mickey Phillips?

Two other items were clipped to the snapshot. A negative, for one. It had been developed carelessly in an amateurish way, as if Wister had done it himself in a borrowed darkroom, or maybe his own kitchen sink.

The other item was a fragment of a newspaper clipping, already going yellow with age. A long banner headline had been folded to fit into the box. It was from his hometown paper and the date was the date of Kathy's murder. The headline read: "FIENDISH KILLERS VANISH." A subhead read: "Terror Strikes Young Wife; Police Baffled." There was a dateline, followed by the first words of the lead: "The home of Mickey Phillips ..." The rest of the story had been torn away and he guessed it would have gone on to say, "a detective on the police force."

He brooded over it a long time without constructive result. He slept off and on. The last time he woke, he was startled to see it was full daylight outside. The photograph and clipping had slipped out of his hand to the floor. He picked it up, studied it briefly, then put it away in his money belt. It was after seven o'clock and he knew that Teller and his man Harry would show up at almost any time. He thought about that for a while, got up and went quietly into the bedroom. He took the key to the strongbox from his pocket and laid it on the floor of the wardrobe, in plain sight. Margarita had been asleep when he entered, but as he started out, she murmured. He looked around and she was watching him from the bed, drowsy and quiescent, one naked arm dangling over the edge. He leaned over and kissed her quickly.

"Good morning, Margarita."

Her eyes swung slowly to look up at him.

"Is *mañana* now, Joe?"

The Venetian blinds were closed beside the bed and he opened one of them to let in a little light.

"We'll go now," he said. "I'll take your things to my car *chiquito automóvil*. When you're dressed, we'll go."

He saw uncertainty in her face.

"We don't tell them?" she said. "Who take care—clean up the place?"

"That's Señor Teller's problem," he said. "No more *trabajo* for Margarita."

He cupped her chin with his hand and kissed her mouth softly.

"Okay, Margarita?"

Her dark eyes shifted, returned, came to rest.

"Okay, Joe," she said.

He carried her bundle outside and down to his garage and put it in the car. He went into his own room and packed his suitcase hurriedly. He started out with it, paused, changed his mind and laid the bag on the luggage rack. He was backing out of the garage when Margarita came along the veranda, wearing the bulky coat and the scarf over her head. He helped her into the car and she checked carefully to make sure he had put the bundle in it. Seeing it in the tonneau seemed to reassure her. She sat quietly beside him, looking straight ahead as he drove onto the highway and turned east toward Yuma. He put his hand on hers where it lay on her thigh.

"You will be all right, Margarita," he said.

"Okay, Joe," she said.

He remembered a cluster of motels near the state line and he drove to the nearest one as fast as he dared. It was called The Swallows, and not till he turned in to the drive did he make any explanation to Margarita.

"We will stop here for a while," he said. "Then we will go to Yuma and find a nice place—a *casa*."

"*Sí*," she said.

He registered as Mr. and Mrs. Marine and got a key to a double room toward the back. The place was not as well kept as the Yucca Tree, but the room was spacious and airy, with twin beds, a large dressing room and full bath. At the Yucca Tree there had been only showers and he saw Margarita gazing at the bathtub.

"*El baño*," she said softly. "*Grande*."

"*Sí*," he said. "*Bueno?*"

"*Bueno*."

He unbuttoned her heavy coat and tossed it aside.

"We'll get you a new coat," he said. "Are you hungry now?"

"No, Joe. Not 'ungry."

"I have to go back to the motel for a short time," he said. "When I come back, we'll have lunch." He took some money out of his pocket and put it in her hand. "Here is some money, if you need it. If you get hungry before I come back, there's a restaurant up on the highway—"

"*Sí*. Not 'ungry, Joe."

"All right. You mustn't be afraid now. I'll lock the

door when I go out and hang this sign on it. Nobody will come in. Okay?"

She nodded.

"I'll come back. You rest now."

"Okay, Joe."

He kissed her nose and mouth and held her for a moment. Then he showed her how the lock worked on the door and went out, hanging the DO NOT DISTURB sign on the outside knob. When he glanced back from the car, she was peering out at him through the blind slats.

A large, expensive car was drawn up near the Yucca Tree office. Mickey decided it must be Teller's car. He went to his room. From inside, through the window, he watched a guest approach the office, enter and come out again, gesticulating mildly. Teller's big frame filled the doorway. The guest turned away and the door closed. Mickey picked up his suitcase and walked down there. When he went in, Teller loomed over the small desk, opening and closing drawers. A beading of sweat laced the curve of his upper lip. His eyes behind the glasses were not readable, but his face wore the usual genial-host creases.

"Mr. Marine!" he said. "Nice to see you. Afraid we're a little off balance here at the moment. What can I do for you?"

"I'm checking out," Mickey said. "I just stopped in to let the young lady know."

"Sorry to see you go. The, uh, young lady seems to have vanished."

"Anything wrong?" Mickey asked.

"No, no. Typical, undependable Mexican help." His hand brushed air over the desk. "Was there any settlement to be made? The motel was Frenchy Wister's enterprise. Afraid I'm not up on the details. My bookkeeper was here, but he left."

"No settlement," Mickey said. "You'll find I'm paid up."

"Don't even mention it, Mr. Marine. No indeed. Hope you enjoyed your stay. Have a good, safe trip."

"I may be around the inn for a few days," Mickey said. "I'm moving into Yuma."

"Good. We'll be glad to see you any time."

Mickey nodded, starting out.

"Goodbye, Mr. Marine," Teller said. "Sorry we couldn't get together at the poker table."

"Yeah," Mickey said.

He put the suitcase in the car and made a quick last-minute survey of the room. He hadn't left anything. He drove out to the highway, swinging east toward Yuma. He drove about half a mile, stopped short of the village limits at Vista del Sol and backed into a byroad. He waited two or three minutes and a moderately long stream of traffic approached, moving west. He worked his way into it and drove back to the motel and beyond it about a quarter mile. He turned onto the gravel drive of an abandoned service station and left the car, partially screened by the gutted service shed. He walked back along the highway.

A high board fence marked the west boundary of the motel property and the building was set back three or four feet from the line, leaving an ample passage. He had looked out at the fence when he had opened the blinds in Margarita's room that morning.

His feet made little sound on the hard-packed ground. Momentarily, as he moved in from the highway toward the passage, he would be in sight from both the kitchen and the living room of Wister's apartment, but it was a chance he had to take and he didn't hesitate. He paused briefly after passing the corner of the building, then moved on between the wall and the fence to the bedroom window.

He stood for some time near the window, listening. At first there was silence. Then he heard the woody grind of sliding doors. From his experience in the room, he knew the sound came from the far side, opposite the window. He moved his face carefully to a point from which he could look through the blind slats. There was no light in the room and it was bright where he stood but after a moment his eyes adjusted to the contrast and he could see.

It was Teller, on his knees, crouched over the strongbox, using the key on it. The lid went up and a big hand filled the box. Mickey watched as it emerged, clutching a sheaf of documents. He leafed through them hastily. He was turned away, presenting a quarter profile and his face contorted as he searched. It occurred to Mickey that it hadn't taken long for him to find the box.

Or maybe he had known where it was and had been constrained from searching by the knowledge that a living Wister would surely know who had been at it. The loss of a snapshot and a negative would diminish the threat to the accessory only slightly.

Accessory. The dry, legalistic word shocked him. After

all that had happened—now, as he felt himself near the end of the long hunt—how could he look calmly through a window at the man who very likely had ordered the murder of his wife, and think no more than "accessory"? Had he grown soft, too flabby to go on with it? Had he changed in some important way, deep inside, where a man's motives are forged?

He shook off the plaguing doubts and watched Teller with the box. The big man had tossed the papers aside and was searching again with his fingers. He lifted out a sheet of cardboard, looked at both sides of it and flung it away. He lifted the empty box slowly, holding it in his two meaty hands, and gazed into it, unbelievingly. His mouth twisted, forming soundless words. He turned the box upside down and shook it, gently at first, then savagely. Crouched on the floor hugely, dwarfing every other object in the room, his hands clutching the box, he was a gigantic grotesque, almost ludicrous, like a monstrous child in a fury over an errant toy. He held it upside down for a long moment, his body quivering with frustration. Then with a vicious downward sweep of his arms, he slammed it to the floor at his knees. Distraught now, he began beating the floor, lifting the box and slamming it down, with a furious, measured rhythm, over and over, as if the box had a life that could be destroyed, as a man's life—or a woman's.

Mickey turned from the window and walked back to his car. The sun was shining brightly, but a cold wind blew off the desert and he hunched his shoulders against it. So it was Teller, he thought. Certainly, beyond a reasonable doubt, it was Teller. All that remained was to confront him with it, force him to admit it—and learn the why of it.

His fist struck painfully against the doorsill of the car. *This* was the time. The man had been asking for it, there on his knees with the damnation of the box in his hands, already disintegrating. And he had walked away from it. Why?

But he knew the answer as he formed the question. To have walked in on Teller at the moment would have been, at even odds, to court disaster. The man was huge, overwrought. In a sudden hand-to-hand combat, Mickey could not count on winning. And if he had tried and lost, Margarita, torn from one accustomed, if dreary, way of life and now suspended short of the promise of the next, would have been a loser, too. There was an old rule about innocent bystanders.

He did some more thinking after he had started the car and turned toward Yuma. As he recovered from the disappointment of the empty box, Teller would begin to think. One of the things he might think would be that Wister had had an arrangement with Margarita to dispose of the incriminating evidence, or to turn it over to someone else. Thinking thus, a reasoning man, driven to the wall, would start looking for Margarita.

Approaching the entrance to the Swallows Motel, he had to slow down from seventy miles an hour to make the turn. The DO NOT DISTURB sign hung as he had left it. He could hear nothing through the door as he searched his pockets for the key he had taken with him. He found it and made it work in the lock.

He pushed inside, took one step and halted, then leaned back heavily, his shoulders pushing the door to. He was panting and choking a little, his throat caught between sobs and laughter. Because he could see Margarita now, through the open dressing room door, on her hands and knees, scrubbing the bathroom floor.

Later, he couldn't remember getting across the room. But he remembered having arrived, being on his knees, the startled Margarita awkwardly sprawled in his arms, smelling of soap and water, while he murmured over and over.

"*Pobrecita, mi pobrecita—*"

And he could remember thinking, Where in hell did I pick up that "*probrecita*"? I must have seen it in a movie.

But Margarita was not celluloid. She was warm flesh and firm muscle and hard bone in his arms. He picked her up, carried her into the bedroom and put her down on one of the beds. He covered her with a spread from the other bed and, kneeling beside her, he explained about the scrubbing of floors.

She listened passively, her large eyes veiled as he talked. When he finished there was a long silence and then she said, "But, Joe—w'at I do?"

"Do! There's plenty to do! You can—wash the dishes—fix things to eat—*enchiladas, frijoles*—"

"*Sí.*"

"You can—I don't know—brush your hair, take a bath, get up, go to bed, go to the movies—"

"Movies? *Cine?*"

"You like the movies?"

"Oh, *sí*. But no movie in *mi pueblo*. I go one time in Nogales, with Señor Wister. And in Guadalajara."

"Who do you like best in the movies? *Mas grande* movie star?"

She pondered seriously.

"*Hombre?*" she said.

"*Sí. Hombre*."

"Ah—Rock 'udson, I think?"

"Okay. We'll find a Rock Hudson movie."

She lay quietly, watching him. He kissed her and, as before, she responded slowly, but with growing warmth, grew restless, clinging, her body arching tautly in his arms. At length, with casual directness, leading him to a natural function uncomplicated by mystique, she took his hand and drew it beneath the thin cover.

"Margarita—?"

"*Sí*."

It was a hissing urgent sound. Her eyes were closed and he saw her nostrils dilate, squeeze taut and dilate again in a rhythmic accompaniment to her breathing, that had a guttural quality in her throat. She was supple and active under him and he was with her a long time, mostly in silence, except at the start when, clutching him, she murmured, "*Poco a poco*, Joe, *por favor—*"

And near the end, in a slow, low-pitched cry of mingled pain and ecstasy, "Ah—Joe!"

16

It had taken most of the day to find a house. He had finally settled on a small, detached cottage near what appeared to be the Mexican quarter. It was one of a group of recently remodeled units around a court, but the one he had rented faced on the street and there was a small park across the way. One reason he had chosen it was that it could be rented by the week and he didn't expect to stay long. Another good feature was the absence of a resident manager.

There had been little time for shopping, but they had been able to get her a few necessities before the stores closed. Then they had stopped at a huge supermarket and stocked up on groceries. Now, having eaten, he sat in a large, comfortable armchair in the living room, looking out through the big front window toward the park across the street.

Margarita was in the bedroom, trying on her new clothes. Unlike Irene, she was shyly grateful, almost awed by them. Another difference was that Margarita required privacy for making changes. From time to time she would come in diffidently and let him look at a blouse-skirt ensemble, or show him how the new shoes looked.

That night, he didn't go to the inn. Despite his reasonable mental assertion that one more day wouldn't make much difference, he felt as if he were shirking a hard duty and be was restless and wakeful most of the night.

The next morning they finished the shopping. He got her a suitcase and, among other things, a garter belt, after he learned she had been trying to keep her stockings up by tying strings around her thighs.

"If you need anything," he explained, "you must ask me. I'm sorry I forgot about the garters."

In an unusual display of her feelings, she framed his face in her hands and kissed him.

"How about going on a picnic?" he said.

"*Que es*—'peek-neek'?"

"It's when you take food somewhere and eat it—out. Like in the desert or the woods."

She looked "out" and thought it over.

"*Sí,*" she said. "*Bueno.*"

He found a place where he could buy barbecued chicken and they drove into the Arizona countryside. He was surprised to find it so different from the vast, barren desert in California. Here there were steep canyons and rugged rock formations, but between one canyon and another stretched broad, irrigated valleys and there were many ranches.

"It's a beautiful country," he said, as they were eating the chicken in a secluded canyon.

"*Sí,*" she said. "*Mi pueblo*—my village in Mexico—is beautiful. *Grande cerros*—what you call?"

She waved toward the high, distant rocks.

"Rocks? Mountains?"

"*Sí, montanas.* But not *rojo* like here. *Blanco.*"

"White?"

"*Sí.*"

"What is the name of your pueblo?"

"*Nuestro pueblo del cerro blanco.*"

"Our town by the white mountain. That's a nice name. How many people in your village?"

"Very small—*hombres, cien*—'undred. *Mujeres, mas*—" She shrugged. "*Chicos*, little ones, *muchos*. Señor Alvarez—big man, *casa grande—el es espagnol*." She lifted her head, speaking with quiet pride. "*Mi*— I am *espagnol*, too, a little. But more India, you know?"

He took her in his arms.

"I know, Margarita," he said. "Do you ever get homesick for your pueblo? You want to go home?"

She looked away.

"Sometime, maybe."

"You want to stay with me—with Joe?"

"*Sí*. I stay, Joe."

He felt a strong urge to make love to her, but there was no place for her to lie on the rocky ground. On the way home he stopped at a sporting goods store and bought an air mattress. He made no comment, only stuffed it into the back seat, but she must have recognized it, because she sat very stiffly for some time and wouldn't look back there.

On the way home they passed a large intersection where the highway west curved off into the desert. He took that fork and drove to a turnout where he pulled off the road. They sat in silence, watching the sun set over the rose-gold mountains.

A battle raged in his divided mind. Unless he could bring himself to give the whole thing up, he would have to finish the job on Teller. He knew it would haunt him if he left it unfinished, but aside from that, it was a thing that had to be done. He was the only one who could do it now. With Roberts and Wister both dead, there was nothing on Teller except Mickey's unsupported word. The case against Teller was inside the man himself, and no official authority could help drag it out of him. Only he alone, Mickey Phillips, could do it. It would mean resuming his nightly vigil at the inn. With luck, it would take only a few more days. But he would have to arrange something about Margarita, to avoid leaving her alone and frightened in the house.

The solution came to him as they were eating dinner. He said nothing about it until they finished and washed the dishes. Then, at eight-thirty, he sat down in the big chair and drew her to his lap.

"Margarita, *chiquita*," he said, "would you like to go to the movies tonight? Rock Hudson?"

"Oh *sí!*"

"I have to go to the inn," he said. "I will take you to the movie and when I get back from the inn, I will pick you up."

"Me alone?" she said.

"Yes, but not for long. You won't have to be alone in the house. Okay?"

She hesitated, then nodded slowly.

"Okay, Joe."

There was no Rock Hudson picture in town, but he finally found a large theater in a well-lighted district where, according to the marquee, a Rock Hudson movie would start the next night. Margarita was disappointed.

"Jimmy Stewart," he said, "*bueno*. Jimmy Stewart *grande* movie star."

"No Rock 'udson?" she said.

"*Mañana*, Rock Hudson."

"Okay, Joe."

The theater was half full. He sat with her for a couple of minutes, then put his mouth to her ear.

"I must go now," he said. "You stay. You will be safe here. Do not go until I come back. *Comprende?*"

"*Sí*, okay, Joe," she whispered tensely.

He saw that she wanted him to leave her undisturbed with the picture. He kissed her cheek quickly and went out. He checked the schedule and saw that the last show would end at twelve-forty-five. He walked to his car and drove away, heading for the inn.

It was a slow night and Charley seemed glad to see him.

"Whole joint's a drag," he said sourly.

"No excitement?" Mickey said.

"I don't know what you call excitement, but that son of a bitch Teller has been on a big prod for anyway two days. Drivin' everybody nuts. Like last night, I'm back here minding my own business, what there is of it, and Teller comes in and sits down at the bar. He glares at me for a while like he could kick my teeth in and then he says, 'Make me a brandy Alexander.' So I make him a goddamn brandy Alexander and then, having nothing else to do, I stand there watching him drink it. And all the time he's giving me that damn eye, you know? Well, it got me sore. I surprised myself. I started looking back at him and pretty soon I said, 'Mr. Teller, I don't get a hell of a lot of call for brandy Alexanders, so if there's anything wrong with that

one, you have my permission to throw it in my face.'
Then I stood around shaking in my socks for the next
two hours, waiting for him to throw me in my own
face. But he didn't and I guess I still got the lousy
job."

"Maybe he's upset about his ex-wife coming back to
take over," Mickey said.

"Maybe."

"Anybody got any idea when she's due?"

"Not me. I think Homer Bridges knows, but he's not
telling. Not even Teller."

"Be interesting to see what will happen."

"You know what I think?" Charley leaned close over
the bar. "I think if she would have turned up in the
last couple of days, Teller wouldn't have said a word.
He would just have beat her to death with his bare
hands."

"You've got me nervous," Mickey said. "Maybe I
better get out of here myself."

Charley laughed.

"He won't make trouble tonight," he said. "He finally
got a poker game going."

"How long will that go on?"

"All night."

"Deputy sheriffs and all?"

Charley nodded.

He stayed in the bar for a couple of hours and finally
gave up hope of seeing Teller that night. As the time
dragged on, his loneliness for Margarita became nearly
unbearable. At eleven-thirty he said good night to
Charley and drove back to the theater.

He found her where he had left her, in a nearly

deserted auditorium. She was wide awake, watching the picture intently. He slid his arm across her shoulders. She moved against him, but would not abandon the movie. He tried to watch it with her, but the screen was extra-large and the figures seemed overpowering. He fell asleep and woke to find her shaking him.

At home she was animated and full of wonder. She told him the story of the movie as she understood it, in a mixture of pantomime and breathless Spanish. He gathered there had been a slinky girl who wore sweaters and was not very nice, and a handsome young man who sat around looking gloomy most of the time and somebody who from time to time got a little drunk. He didn't dare laugh at her and finally swept her into his arms and hugged her till she squealed to be released.

"How did you like Jimmy Stewart?" he asked.

"Jimmee Stewart?" she said. "*Quien es*—Jimmee Stewart?"

He picked her up and took her to bed.

The next evening, having left Margarita to enjoy the Rock Hudson movie, he decided he couldn't wait indefinitely for the "right moment," with Teller. He would have to create the moment, make it happen. He worked it out carefully in his mind. He had mentioned to Teller that he was moving to Yuma. He would force a conversation with him. He would tell him, casually, as if by the way, that he had run into the Mexican girl who had worked for Wister. He would say he had talked to her and she had shown him this envelope she had found among her things after she had left. She thought it belonged to Señor Wister and she didn't know what to do with it. He would then say that he had offered to relieve her of it and deliver it to Mr. Teller, who would know what to do about it. So she had let him have it, but unfortunately he had forgotten to pick it up before coming to the inn this evening. He would try to remember it the next time; or, if Teller should happen to be in Yuma, he could drop by at Mickey's place and pick it up. He would give Teller the address of the *chiquita casa*. It would be safe enough, because he would be there to welcome him. Once he had Teller alone, off home base, he could handle him all right.

He went over the plan step by step, word by word, and could find no flaw in it. By the time he reached the inn he had the good, taut, ready feeling on which he had depended in the past and which he thought he had lost in the frustration over Wister's untimely death. Although there was no more business than on other nights, as he went into the bar, he noticed a different mood among the help. There was a sense of relaxation. Even Charley was whistling quietly when Mickey sat down and ordered his whisky and water.

"What happened?" he asked. "Somebody get promoted?"

Charley winked sardonically.

"The cat's away," he said. "The big boss, he is gone."

Mickey's hand caressed the cold glass stiffly.

"Mr. Teller?" he said.

"Who else?"

Then Charley was called away and Mickey sat with

the new frustration, his throat squeezed too tight to drink, listening to the sly jokes passing among the few off-the-street guests and the help.

"Yeah," Charley said happily, returning. "Said he was going all the way to Los Angeles."

"Oh," Mickey said carefully. "Then he'll be back."

"Sure. But not tonight, friend. Tomorrow."

Mickey drew a long breath. It could have been worse. Teller might have taken off for good.

Charley brought him another drink before he had half finished the first.

"On the house," Charley said. "That is—" he pointed—"on Mr. Bridges."

"Hey, Mr. Marine!" a voice called behind him.

He turned on the stool and the little manager was half standing in one of the big booths beckoning him. He got down from the bar and went over there. Homer beamed up at him.

"You're the steadiest customer we've had here for a month," he said. "Sit down and have a drink."

"Thanks," Mickey said, sitting down in the booth. "I'm still working on one Charley gave me—on you."

"Good old Charley," Homer said.

A nice little guy, Mickey thought. In spite of his short, spare frame and his mannerisms around the place, he was a nice little guy when you sat down with him.

"I suppose Charley told you the reason for this—uh—relaxation, too," he said.

"He mentioned Mr. Teller had gone away."

"Wouldn't want you to think," the little man said, clearing his throat, "we do this every day. Have to admit, though, it's a relief."

His eyes grew thoughtful, reminiscent.

"Mr. Marine," he said, "I've been with this place ever since it opened, more than three years ago. The Tellers—that is, Mrs. Teller actually—took over a rundown, jinxed desert hotel and made it go!"

After a while Mickey said, "I heard Mrs. Teller is due back here any day."

Bridges looked around carefully.

"You heard about the divorce, I take it," he said.

"A little."

"Horrible," he muttered. "It was like living in hell here for a few weeks. But it was the only thing they could do. You talk about a mismatched couple—they had nothing in common. Nothing!" He cleared his throat lightly. "I happened to be present one evening in a group of hilarious guests, all of whom were friends of Mrs. Teller's, and one of them asked, 'Honey, how did you ever come to take up with a son of a bitch like Fred Teller?' Her reply, as I recall, was, 'Honey, I was young and a little on the cocky side. I saw this guy and made a bet with myself. I bet I could tame that big bear. I lost.'"

"But she didn't lose the inn."

"No. She had her own money in it and most of her own ideas. She let him have everything else and gave him a year to get out of the inn. She was generous."

"How did Mr. Teller take it?"

"Very hard. I saw him with my own eyes—after the divorce—I saw him sit right here in this booth and cry, tears running down his face, talking about how he'd worked and sweated and planned to build the

Montezuma Inn and all he got for it was a kick in the teeth. Well, if you'll excuse the expression, Mr. Marine, that was nothing but a lot of crybaby crap. *She* built this place. She ran it. I tell you, when she was here, this was the best spot of its kind between the Mexican border and Las Vegas. People had fun here. She was a natural hostess, the greatest. Will be again."

Bridges craned his neck to look over the top of the booth, then pulled a postcard from his pocket.

"Here's the reason I'm celebrating tonight," he said. "This came today. You're welcome to real it. May give you an idea what she's like."

Mickey glanced at the view side of the card. It looked vaguely familiar, but he didn't place it at once and flipped the card over. There was a brief message:

"There ain't no Bluebird of Happiness east of Yuma. See you soon. Love. M."

Bridges was saying something, but Mickey couldn't hear it. He was staring at the postmark. The card had been mailed from his home city. He turned it over again. Now he recognized the view, a monument in the principal park of the city. He had played in its shadow as a boy. As a policeman, he had once cornered two thieves near it.

He handed the card to Bridges.

"It's from her hometown," Bridges said. "Some small city in Illinois. She went back there for a while right after the divorce. Didn't stay long. She went to Europe. She's been traveling mostly ever since."

"Did Mr. Teller know where she was all the time?"

He realized, as he said it, it was not the kind of question he ought to ask, but the little manager, caught up in his memories and anticipations, took it casually.

"No, I'm sure he didn't. Oh, he knew she went back home right after the divorce. There were details, you know, and their attorneys sending stuff back and forth. But she didn't keep in touch with Teller personally." He lowered his voice. "Tell you the truth, I think she was a little afraid of him. He's a dangerous man in some ways, vengeful—and he has odd tastes."

"May I ask you a personal question?" Mickey said.

"Sure. Go ahead."

"How is it that after Mrs. Teller went away—?"

Bridges stopped him with a gesture.

"I know what you're going to ask," he said. "Why did I stay? That's simple. I was part of the settlement."

Mickey stared at him.

"Well," Bridges said defensively, "a child can be included in a divorce settlement; why not a manager of what you own? Someone to look after your interests."

"I see."

Bridges glanced at the postcard and slipped it into his pocket.

"I noticed she signed it with just an initial," Mickey said. "You knew who it was from all right?"

"Oh certainly." Bridges was divided now, his alert eyes on some subtle shift in conditions in the direction of the lobby, unnoticeable to Mickey. "Her maiden name," he went on absently, "was Phillips. Michelline Phillips. Everybody called her Mickey."

Suddenly he was on his feet, gazing toward the lobby.

"Christ," he said, "it never stops. Excuse me, Mr.

Marine, nice to talk to you."

"Yes," Mickey said. "Thanks for the drink."

Bridges scurried away and disappeared. Mickey stared down at his stiff fingers lying on the littered table.

So it all fits, he thought. It's all there now. It was Mrs. Teller's hometown and she was heading there and Teller knew it. And her name was Mickey Phillips.

He lingered a while, so as not to appear too interested in Teller's absence. But he left earlier than usual and when he picked Margarita up, she left with him readily, even though the first showing of the Rock Hudson movie wasn't finished. Driving home, they agreed that the next day would be a good one for a picnic.

But the next day, it rained. Mickey was just as glad. Sealed in the house with her, he felt secure, stabilized. He found her endlessly fascinating. She had organized her new wardrobe with ceremonial precision. She had a breakfast and dishwashing outfit, an outfit for cleaning the house, another for afternoon. Between changes, she nearly always bathed herself completely. He didn't try to modify her obsessive cleanliness, but he was determined to teach her the enjoyment of leisure.

She could not be idle. He guessed that if he didn't interrupt her from time to time, sometimes by sheer force, she would go on from dawn to bedtime without a break. On that rainy afternoon, following a short nap, he had found her busily scrubbing the floor of the service porch where rain had seeped in under the screen door. He picked her up in both arms and carried her into the living room, put her on his lap. After a while her restlessness ebbed and she lay warmly against him.

"A little *trabajo*—a little rest," he said. "All *trabajo*—no fun—very bad. *Malo.*"

"*Sí,*" she said.

He kissed her and she snuggled deep in his lap.

"Tell me about your village," he said.

She told him, haltingly at first, then warming to it as she remembered. She remembered with fondness and he found himself caught up in the atmosphere she evoked. The picture of bucolic peace in a remote, primitive village appealed to him strongly. He would go there with her, right away after he had finished with Teller. He would find a way to fit in there, work with his hands, make a home for them.

"No picnics in your village?" he asked idly.

"No. *Fiesta, sí*, but no peekneek."

"You like picnics?"

"*Sí.* No peekneek today. Rain."

"Well, we can have a picnic right here in the house."

"Oh, Joe—"

"*Sí.* I fix. You make sandwiches."

"W'at kind sandwiches?"

"*Tortilla* sandwiches."

"*Tacos?*"

"*Sí*, plenty *tacos.*"

While she made the *tacos*, he spread a tablecloth on the floor of the living room and did some rearranging of the furniture. When she came in to see what he was doing she stared, openmouthed. He explained it, item by item.

"Tree," he said, pointing to the floor lamp.

He upended the big armchair.

"Mountain," he said. "*Cerro.*"

"Oh Joe—"

He put a sofa cushion on the floor for her to sit on.

"Rock," he said. He got another. "*Dos* rocks. Rocks better for seat than head."

She began to laugh.

"Joe, you crazy," she said.

"*Sí,*" he said. "Where are the *tacos?*"

She brought them and they sat on the cushions, eating. She had got into the spirit and laughed often. When they finished the *tacos*, he sat for some minutes in quiet rumination, then jumped up suddenly.

"I forgot the most important thing," he said. "You stay; I'll be back."

She watched him go outside and run to the car, parked in the street, his shoulders hunched against the rain. When he came in with the air mattress under his arm, she began to look askance. It took him some time to inflate it, on his knees on the floor, huffing and puffing and getting red in the face. Not till she began laughing again did he realize what a ludicrous picture he made. He started to laugh with her, lost his grip on the air nozzle and watched the mattress collapse with a long, shuddering sigh. When he got over the laughing, he picked her up and carried her into the bedroom.

She gazed up at him, drowsy and fulfilled.

"Joe," she murmured, "this too is peekneek?"

"*Sí*," he said.

She smiled slowly.

"Peekneek—*muy bueno*," she said.

He was reaching for her when he heard what sounded like a knock on the front door. The rain was making a clatter on the frame building and he couldn't be sure. He got up and opened the bedroom door, listening. The sound came again, louder, unmistakably a knocking. When he turned back into the room and reached for his trousers and a shirt, Margarita stared up at him tensely. He smiled.

"It's okay," he said. "You stay here. I tell them to *vamos*."

Barefooted, he left the room, closing the door behind him. The living room was neat enough except for the mess he had made himself. He tossed the cushions onto the sofa, picked up the tablecloth and stuffed it under the cushions and kicked the flabby air mattress into a corner. He headed for the door, but stopped short of it abruptly.

He had gone through this once before, in almost precisely the same way. The memory came back so sharply he caught his breath in quick pain. His facial muscles reacted to the savage blow; his stomach contracted violently.

But Roberts and Wister were dead....

After a moment he moved aside and looked slantwise through the window toward the door. He could see an arm and shoulder bundled in a raincoat, part of a hat. He couldn't see who it was. He was pretty sure it was only one. There was no car parked out front. If it were somebody from Immigration, he thought, there would be a car.

He moved to the door, crouched near it with knee and shoulder braced to repel a forced entry, and opened it far enough to look outside. The caller was standing with head down. He glanced up as the door opened. Mickey inhaled slowly, trying to keep the breath from running wild in his throat. Then he opened the door fully, watching the old, familiar, half-forgotten and now suddenly recalled face of Captain Andrews.

17

Not until the Captain had taken off his coat and hat, with a grumbled apology, and Mickey had put them in the kitchen near the stove to dry and had returned to the living room did they greet each other. The Captain looked disgruntled and uncomfortable, which, as Mickey recalled, was normal.

"Hello, Phillips," he said, extending a wiry hand.

"Captain," Mickey said.

They shook hands stiffly.

"Well," Mickey said, "sit down."

The Captain sat on the edge of a chair with his hands between his knees. He gave the house a pretty thorough casing, but Mickey couldn't tell what he saw.

"How are things back home?" Mickey asked.

"Stumbling along," the Captain said. "Meyer got in an accident a couple of weeks ago. Run over by his own car. He was washing it and forgot to set the brakes."

"Hurt bad?"

"You can't hurt Meyer. He's got a slight limp."

Mickey couldn't think of any more homey questions. His mind churned with other kinds of questions, but he decided to let the Captain get to it in his own way. The Captain seemed reluctant. He spread his hands out, backs up, and looked at them, rubbed them together between his knees, sat back with his legs crossed, then came forward again to the edge of the chair.

"Uh—Mickey," he said, "I guess I better get down to cases. The way it goes kind of depends. To start at the beginning, when you asked me for a leave of absence, I figured that you wanted to go hunting a couple of guys, like I might have done in your shoes. But I couldn't give you a leave of absence and you left anyway, which kind of hurt me at the time, but that's all past. So I figured, again, that you would probably go on your manhunt anyway, on your own. Now if that's what you did and if you're still on it, that's what we have to talk about. If not, if you just went off and did something else, that's none of my business—or anybody else's—and we can pass the time of day and I'll go back home."

It was Mickey's turn to look at his hands.

"Well," the Captain said after a minute, "have you been working on the case?"

"Yes," Mickey said, looking up. "I have."

"Tell me what you got."

It was so characteristic, so familiar, that Mickey almost felt himself to be back on the job, in the squad room or the Captain's office. Captain Andrews always, unquestionably, had been in charge.

"Well, Captain," Mickey said, "I have some questions of my own."

"Sure," the Captain said. "I'll answer any question you ask, if I know the answer, but I've got to hear from you first."

You could always take the Captain's word. It wouldn't do any good to stall or try to hold out. The Captain had come a long way, and somewhere he had a good, solid reason.

"All right," Mickey said, getting up. "Just give me a minute."

He went to the bedroom, opened the door enough to slide inside and closed the door when he was in. Margarita was sitting cross-legged on the bed, naked, and her eyes were like ripe olives, watching him. He smiled, forcing it, and picked up his money belt from the chair where he had tossed it. He didn't try to hide from her that he removed the photograph and clipping she had given him at the motel. He leaned over the bed and kissed her.

"Joe—" she whispered urgently. "Poleecy?"

"It's okay," he said. "*Amigo.* Good friend."

He turned away quickly and returned to the living room. He handed the photo and clipping to the Captain, who winced at the picture, then sat holding it, waiting for Mickey to go on.

"There was this guy," Mickey said, "Frenchy Wister ..."

It didn't take long to tell it—from his arrival in Vista del Sol, with a passing reference to Margarita, to his examination of the county records, his discovery of

Teller at Wister's strongbox and the coincidence of Mrs. Teller's maiden name. When he finished, he saw that the Captain knew he had only a piece of the story, but for reasons of his own was letting it pass for the time being.

"And this Wister is dead?" the Captain said.

"Yes sir."

"And the big fella, Teller, he's away?"

"That's right. But he'll be back."

The Captain looked at the wisps of film and newsprint in his hand and made a gesture of hopelessness.

"And this is the evidence?" he said.

"Yes."

"Did anybody see you find it in Wister's box?"

"No," Mickey said.

"Anybody besides you see Mr. Teller going through the box?"

"No."

The Captain sighed heavily.

"I didn't have much choice, Captain," Mickey said. "If I hadn't taken it out of Wister's box, Teller would have taken it and we wouldn't even have this much. Wister was dead and I had to move fast."

"Well, there's still the property deal on the county records. Nobody can change that. Go ahead. What do you think happened?"

"I think it was like this," Mickey said. "Teller was going to lose the inn here to his divorced wife, if she came back to claim it. It was probably set up so that if she never claimed it, he would keep it. Somebody would have to keep it. Anyway, Teller knew she was going back to her hometown. He had this hungry oddball hanging around, Frenchy Wister, and he made him a deal. Half of the motel wouldn't be much to pay for insurance that Mrs. Teller would never show up to claim the inn. But it would look pretty good to Wister, who was a gambler and probably hungry most of the time."

"Why would Wister do it like this?" Andrews cut in, glancing at the picture. "Why this weird stuff?"

"I don't know. It might have been his own idea, for kicks. Or he might have wanted to make it look good to Teller, who is on the weird side himself. Or Teller might have ordered it that way, so the victim would make no mistake who was behind it."

"But Wister didn't kill Mrs. Teller. He killed— somebody else. You mean to tell me that when he turned up this picture, as proof he'd done the job, Teller wouldn't know the difference?"

"Teller," Mickey said, "like other people, is shrewd in some ways and stupid in others. He was stupid to hire a killing, put himself on the hook. Maybe he didn't think of it at the time, but he would have thought it over by the time Wister got back. Wister would have a bad thing on him the rest of his life. So even if he knew Wister had got the wrong one, he wouldn't have much choice but to pay off and shut up. It would be foolish to try again. It's true you can only hang once, but if you kill twice, you're twice as likely to get caught."

The Captain's fist, clutching the meager evidence, thudded on his thigh.

"But why—why Kathy Phillips!"

"I don't know," Mickey said. "We lived in the country—it was convenient. Wister probably scouted around town. When he couldn't find Mrs. Teller—who had moved on by then—being desperate and hungry, he started looking for somebody else—anybody."

"But you said that when you answered the door that night, they asked you, 'Does Mickey Phillips live here?'"

"A name, Captain. The name was on the mailbox, in the phone book. I think Wister never saw Mrs. Fred 'Mickey Phillips' Teller. Maybe he thought Kathy was the one. Even after he found out different, he had Teller over the same barrel. Teller had to pay off."

The Captain got up, turned to the window and looked out at the rain.

"Well," he said, "we've got enough to pick Teller up for questioning. I guess the local men will cooperate—"

"Captain, it won't work," Mickey said. "The local police are friendly with Teller. They might cooperate, but routine questioning won't do it. The only case against Teller is in his head."

The Captain's back stiffened.

"You mean we have to sweat it out of Teller informally—what they call extralegally?"

"I mean *I* do, Captain."

The Captain turned slowly.

"The way you sweated it out of that other one—Roberts—in Colorado?" he said.

Mickey stared at him.

"How do you think I caught up with you?" Captain Andrews said. "Why do you think I'm here?"

"I was going to ask—"

"I started a while back. I got a call from a police officer in Chicago, the one showed you the mug shots. He said he gave you a batch of old APB's and you told him your man wasn't in them. So he was running through them later and he came across this Lou 'The Barber' Roberts. On a hunch he called me. I checked with Kansas City and they said Roberts had blown town."

"Captain—"

"Let me finish! I checked some more. I got a make on Roberts from Denver. I got one on you, from some hotel dick that didn't like you. I went to Denver. I missed you by a few hours, but I had a talk with that broad in the hotel. I tailed her to the airport. But I lost you after you left.

"The only lead I had was to Las Vegas, where we knew Roberts had spent some time. But I figured if you were going to Las Vegas, you'd have got on the plane with the broad. I went back to do some checking with the Denver police and—a thing happened."

The Captain went out of focus. Mickey shook his head.

"What—happened—Captain?"

"A report came down out of the mountains. That old hotel up there—the fire went out. Couple of guys up there knew somebody was at the hotel. But the fire was out! They started nosing around. They found Lou Roberts in that mine shaft, where you dumped him."

Mickey stood silent, waiting.

"So I was back with my Las Vegas lead," the Captain said. "The Denver police got out bulletins on you everywhere. There was nothing I could do for them. I knew you were driving, so if you were heading for Las Vegas you'd go the southern route because up north it was all snowed in. I went south out of Denver and west on Sixty-six. I been hanging around this Godforsaken desert for a week, because I got a tip on you around town. I got a description of your car. I been driving up and down every street in town. Today I finally made it."

There was a long pause while they looked at each other.

Then Mickey said, "Have you been in touch with the local police?"

"Yeah."

"What's the score, Captain?"

"You tell me first what the score is. Tell me about Roberts. This is a public police matter and I'm in it."

Mickey wet his lips with his tongue, glanced toward the closed bedroom door and started to talk. He told the Captain everything that had happened with Roberts. It took longer than it had taken to tell the other thing, because he was trying to explain to the Captain how he had felt at the time and it was difficult. The Captain never took his eyes off Mickey's face.

"I killed Roberts in self-defense," Mickey said, finishing it. "I dumped him and left him so there wouldn't be any chance for anybody to tip Wister. I didn't think about the fire going out."

The Captain looked at him a while longer, then turned his back and looked at the rain. Mickey felt a painful, irregular throbbing in his neck.

"How come it wasn't in the papers?" he said finally.

"About Roberts?"

"Because I sweated and argued and fought with the Denver people to keep it out. For the same reason you just gave me."

"But the local police know about it?"

"Yeah, they know. But they haven't found you yet. Only me, I found you."

"Well, Captain, what do you think?"

The Captain turned to face him.

"I believe you," he said. "But I'm only the start. You'll have to go back a long time and convince a lot of people. There's no other way out—unless ..."

"Unless what?"

"We can get it out of Teller. You say he's due back tonight?"

"That's right."

"I can wait a few hours before reporting in—"

"Captain, I have to do it myself."

"You're crazy! Why? Haven't you got the thing out of your system yet?"

"As a practical matter. If you go to the inn with me, somehow Teller will get tipped. He won't show up."

"Why! Tell me why!"

"Because you're a cop. You look and smell like a cop. You're a cop a million miles away!"

"You're not, Phillips? You're not a cop?"

"Not anymore."

The Captain's shoulders sagged. He moved wearily to the big chair, sat down on the edge off it and clamped his hands together tight.

"Then I'll have to take you in and we'll do the best we can with Teller," he said.

"Give me a break, Captain."

"A break? To murder Teller?"

"I won't kill him. Not even in self-defense."

It was a wild, unbelievable statement, he knew the moment the words were out. The Captain's face twisted.

"I've got plenty of reason to live," Mickey said. "Wait just a minute."

He went to the bedroom and inside. She was standing just inside the door and she moved against him at once, full and warm, as if to comfort him. It had grown dark in the room and he could barely see the pale oval of her face. But he could feel her vitality, the wiry-soft, restless thrust, supple and catlike, yet caressing, too, as if she would enfold all of him at once.

"Joe—"

"*Sí, chiquita*," he said gently. "Everything will be all right. *Por favor*, I want the Captain to meet you."

"Poleecy?"

"Old friend. *Amigo*," he said.

"Okay, Joe."

He switched on the light and she fussed at her hair before the mirror and straightened her new skirt. When she slipped her hand under his arm, it was trembling. They went into the next room and the Captain rose slowly, seeing her.

"Captain," Mickey said, "*amigo*, this is Señorita Margarita Sandoval."

The Captain nodded hesitantly. Margarita glanced at Joe, then bowed a little, somewhat awkwardly. She murmured a formal greeting in Spanish.

"Do you like Mexican food?" Mickey asked.

The Captain blinked at him.

"I don't know," he said.

"We will be pleased to have you eat with us," Mickey said. "Okay, Margarita?"

She looked up at him quickly, shyly, then bowed. "*Sí.* Okay, Joe. I fix."

The Captain didn't say much during the meal. When they finished, he thanked Margarita graciously. Margarita was still nervous in his presence, but she had relaxed from her earlier tension, Mickey thought. She excused herself and disappeared in the bedroom. A few minutes later, Mickey saw her peering out through a narrow opening, beckoning him urgently. When he went in to her, she was stiff and anxious. He had no idea how much of his conversation with the Captain she had heard nor how much of that she had understood.

"Joe," she said, "*por favor*, the *cine*—movies—not tonight, huh? You stay tonight?"

He gathered her close, kissed her deeply, holding her till she responded, her mouth warm and mobile against his.

"I must go tonight," he said. "It's the last time. Everything will be all right. Don't be afraid."

"It is a bad thing you do," she said.

"It must be done. Only I can do it."

"Joe, the picture I show you—that woman—"

"*Sí?*"

"Señor Wister do that."

"He told you?"

"*Sí.* He say I stay with him, do like he says, or he do

that to me. He was—crazy—talk funny. How you say?"

"Drunk?"

"*Sí*, very drunk. He tell me Señor Teller make him do it." He led her to the bed, made her sit down. He put his hand over hers in her lap and held them tightly.

"Why didn't you tell me this before?" he asked.

"I was afraid. For you. I don't know w'at you do at the een—with Mr. Teller."

Pretty soon she said, "I was wrong, Joe?"

"It's all right," he said. "Everything will be all right." He sat in silence, thinking about it.

"Joe," Margarita said, "Señor Wister not dead. Last night I see him—at the *cine*."

It took him a while to get the words sorted out in his throat.

"Did he see you?" he said quietly.

"*Sí*, I think so. He look at me long time. I wait for you. When you come, he is not there."

"Are you sure it was Señor Wister?"

"*Sí*, I am sure."

He released her hands and got up. There were two windows in the room. He made sure each one was locked and he lowered the blinds on each. He paused by the bed and touched her arms lightly.

"You stay right here," he said, "while I talk to the Captain. Don't be afraid."

"Okay, Joe," she said.

The trust in her voice was a knife-thrust under his heart as he left the room to tell the Captain what he had learned.

18

The Captain listened calmly.

"So," Mickey said, finishing it up, "it looks as if they rigged the telephone call to make me think Wister was dead."

"They were probably both on to you by the time you got here," the Captain said.

"But how could they know about Roberts?"

"I knew about Roberts. You said Teller had friends on the local police."

"All right. But why go to all that trouble? They could have had me thirty different ways—"

"It might have meant another killing. They just wanted you to go away. They would figure, because of the Roberts thing, you were too hot to do any talking, especially to the law. As far as they knew, you had nothing on Teller. If you thought Wister was dead, maybe you would give up. It could have worked— anyway long enough for both of them to get far away. With his ex-wife coming back to take over, Teller had a logical excuse to disappear."

"Then why not disappear? Why stall around?"

"Because you didn't disappear. And because when Teller went to Wister's strongbox, the evidence was gone. They need that."

Mickey pounded his fist on his knee in helpless fury.

"It was so convincing—him banging that box on the floor. I swallowed the whole pitch—"

"He wasn't acting. Besides, he couldn't have counted

on you watching. Wister probably told him where to look. It must have been quite a shock to him to find the stuff missing. He doubtless guessed you had got hold of it, and he would have to get it back."

"And I took it the way Teller played it. The only break we got was that he didn't know how it was with Margarita and me. If he'd known that, he wouldn't have waited till morning to open that box—"

He broke off. They looked at each other.

"Margarita—" Mickey said.

"They need her, too," the Captain said. "You think they know where she is, for sure?"

"It would have been easy enough for Wister to tail us from the theater last night. They may not know yet that you're here. If they're out there somewhere now, they're probably waiting till the street quiets down, people go to bed ..."

The Captain sat in the big armchair with his head back, looking like a man who had a mildly irritating day at the office and was glad for a little rest.

"What do you think?" he asked after a minute.

Mickey's answer was prompt.

"The first thing to do is to get Margarita in a safe place—like in the hands of Immigration. They'd keep her at least overnight."

"Where are they?" the Captain said.

"I don't know."

"You have a telephone?"

"No."

"Neighbors have a telephone?"

"Maybe."

"Turn off the lights," the Captain said.

Mickey got up, moving casually, and switched off the overhead light and the lamp beside the Captain's chair. The Captain got up, went to the window and stood looking out. After a long time he turned back to the chair.

"Hard to tell," he said. "There's nobody on the street. Can't see anything in that park. It's not raining anymore."

"Captain, do you have a gun?"

"No. I didn't plan to shoot it out with you."

Mickey took his turn at the window, with no better results than the Captain had got. He went across the dark room and into the bedroom, where Margarita was sitting, just as he had left her, her hands curled together in her lap.

"Margarita," he said, "I'm not going out tonight. We'll just stay together. Pretty soon, we'll go for a ride in the car, take the Captain to his hotel. Maybe we'll get some ice cream on the way home."

"*Sí*, okay," she said.

"You wait a minute and I'll go out and start the car. When the Captain says it's time, you come out with the Captain to the car."

"Okay, Joe. I come."

"Better put your coat on, huh? It's cold outside."

"*Sí*."

He disliked using the confidence stuff on her, but it would be easier to explain to her after they got started, about the Immigration people and that he would come and pick her up in Mexico the next day; and it would give her less time to worry about it before it happened.

He went back to the living room and the Captain

was waiting in the dark.

"I'll go out alone to the car," Mickey said. "If it looks clear all around, I'll give you a horn. You bring Margarita out then. Okay?"

"Okay, but let *me* go. They don't want me for anything—"

"They will, if they're out there, when they see you come out of here."

"Well—"

"I'll give you a horn, Captain," Mickey said firmly. "Or I'll come back."

He twisted the knob and opened the door, took a glance outside and went out. There was a thirty-foot walk to the street. The rain had stopped, but the flagstone walk was wet and he could see the wet grass glistening in the faint light from the street lamp, nearly a block away. There were no pedestrians in sight on the street in either direction and he could see nobody on the near edge of the park across the way.

He got into the car, slid under the wheel, found his keys and switched on the ignition. He pressed the starter and nothing happened. It turned over all right, but there was no spark, no igniting. He tried it several times, checked his gasoline supply, which was adequate, and finally knew it was hopeless. He got out, went to the back and saw that the engine hood was unlatched. So they had been at it. He didn't bother to inspect the damage. It would be sufficient to make the car useless.

He looked the street over carefully in both directions. A few cars were parked at long intervals, none but his own near the court where they lived. The parking lot for the court was on the next street and he had never used it. He checked the telephone wires as far as he could see in the darkness. The only line leading to the court ran to a unit toward the back. There were no lights in the house. There was no line to either house next door. A line connected the second house to his left, fifty yards down the street. It was dark, but a car was parked in front of it. He thought he might rouse somebody, or anyway get inside the house. But it was too far. It would be too long to leave the Captain, alone, unarmed, and Margarita

He returned to the house, not hurrying, but not wasting any time either. Before he spoke to the Captain, he went to the kitchen. He hooked the screen door that led outside off the service porch, and he locked the inside kitchen door and closed the blind on its small, square window. It wasn't much of a door, he thought, turning back to the living room.

He stood in the middle of the room and traded looks with the Captain.

"Car won't start," he said.

The Captain nodded.

"I guess we could shade that window," he said, "and turn on a light and see what happens."

Mickey ground his teeth.

"We don't even know if they're out there," he said.

"I know," the Captain said, "but if we were in their shoes, we would be out there, and we know somebody monkeyed with the car. If you want to try it on foot to the nearest well-lighted street, I'll go along. But it's a lot to ask of Margarita."

Mickey pulled down the shade on the front window and switched on the overhead light. It threw harsh shadows over the old, faded wallpaper, the chain-store furniture, the frayed carpet. He cringed at the sight of it, a cheap, threadbare hideout, where he had brought Margarita. And it could turn out to be her tomb—and his, and the Captain's—because he had fouled up. The foul-up with Teller, being outsmarted, manipulated by Teller, was only the last of a series. The big foul-up was the first, when he had walked out on the Captain, to do it himself, alone. Big man!

Because they always came to this cheap, threadbare end. When you used the methods of thief, hoodlum, killer, you became one of them. You could expect to go down like them, and bring others down with you. That would be the hell you went to, living or dying, the faces of the people you had loved and brought down.

He was moving toward the bedroom. He was wondering how he could explain this to Margarita, and ask her forgiveness, in the short, bad time that might remain, when he heard the footsteps outside. He halted, feeling the knot of fear like a hot fist between his shoulder blades. He turned slowly and saw that the Captain had heard, too. They listened together to the soggy, measured tramp of feet on the wet flagstones. There were at least two men.

They reached the door and stopped. Mickey's nails dug sharply at his moist palms. He began to count— one, two, three—in time with his racing pulse. Then the knock came, hard, quick, a staccato bark against the old, cheap panel. The Captain was looking at him from the chair. Mickey moved closer to the door.

"What do you want?" he called.

Up in that hotel in the mountains, Roberts, desperate with fear, had said to him, "What do you want?" ...

One of them outside answered, "Mr. Marine? Joe Marine?"

It was not a voice he had heard before. He glanced at the Captain, who had his hands now on the arms of the chair, gripping. The Captain nodded.

"All right," Mickey said. "What is it?"

"... officers," the voice said. "Bureau of Immigration. Open up."

The sweat of sudden relief washed over him from forehead to shaking knees. His hand groped for the doorknob. But the Captain was up from the chair now, moving past him, and he touched Mickey's arm in passing.

"Easy," he muttered.

Mickey waited until the Captain had stationed himself behind the big chair and was leaning on it in an attitude of casual curiosity, then opened the door slowly, moving back with it, a thin shield from shoulder to toe.

Two men stepped inside. They were of medium height, adequately set up, dressed in trench coats and soft hats. One of them, slightly taller and stockier than the other, did the talking.

"You have a Mexican national here named Margarita Sandoval?" he said.

Mickey closed the door behind them and walked out around them till he stood between them and the bedroom and could watch the Captain, still leaning on the chair a few feet away and slightly to the rear of the nearer of the two. The Captain nodded slightly.

"What if I have?" Mickey said.

"She's in the country illegally," the one said. "We'll have to take her with us."

The Captain shrugged and nodded again.

"Well," Mickey said, "it was bound to happen. She's in the bedroom. I'll ask her to get dressed."

"All right," the one said. "The sooner the better."

Mickey swung as if to turn, then paused, looking at them.

"A—*como se llama, señor?*" he said.

They glanced at each other. The spokesman looked impatient.

"Come on," he said. "We're *American* officers."

Mickey looked at the Captain, who shook his head faintly.

"I happen to be a police officer myself," the Captain said. "You gentlemen won't object to showing some identification, will you?"

The one nearer the Captain, the more slender one, took half a stride back and turned, his knees crowding the armchair seat beside the Captain.

"No objection," he said.

He reached inside his coat. When he brought his hand out, there was a gun in it, stubby and lethal, aimed at the Captain's head, just out of reach over the back of the chair.

"Now let's get the girl," the other one said.

Mickey's hands were cold. He calculated the Captain's chances at zero. His own were slightly better. Margarita's he didn't dare think about.

The stocky one advanced on him, reaching for his

own gun as he came. It was the same as the other.

"Go ahead," he said.

"I'll tell her to get dressed," Mickey said.

He turned his back on the gun and went to the bedroom door, listening to the steps of the one behind him, not too close. He rapped on the door.

"Margarita," he said sharply. "*El baño!*"

The one behind him had stopped. He stood at the door, waiting an endless time, finally heard the bedsprings lurch softly, the gentle padding of her feet toward the bathroom.

"Come on," the stocky one said tightly behind him.

"Give her a chance to get dressed—"

"Never mind that."

Mickey turned, with one hand on the doorknob, and the fellow was out of reach, with the gun leveled. He saw that no change had taken place at the armchair where the Captain leaned, looking into the other gun. Mickey didn't doubt they would use the guns. It would make a disturbance, but by the time any neighbors might rouse, the two of them could be long gone with Margarita. It explained—a flash thought in his mind—why Teller and Wister had waited. They would import this expert help only after careful thought.

The stocky one grimaced.

"Come on," he said. "Don't make me blast you out of the way."

Mickey shrugged, twisted the knob and opened the door into the dark bedroom, stepping back with it quickly to come abreast of the one with the gun. The ruse worked; not for long, but long enough. The stocky one took two steps toward the open doorway before he thought. Then he stopped, but by then Mickey was behind him. He hit him with the heels of both hands, in the small of the back, with all his weight. The guy's head snapped backward; he screamed faintly and fell, clawing, across the room into the wall beside the bed. Mickey heard the violent outbreak behind him as the Captain pushed the big chair into the other one and the gun exploded.

He had fallen on his knees with the impetus of his push into the bedroom. He had heard the gun drop, but it took him some time in the dark to get his hand on it. When he found it, the other one had started up, gasping for breath and was clubbing at him, wild in the dark and in pain. Mickey slashed at him with the gun barrel till he fell away and lay still.

When he got into the lighted living room, the slender one had his knee in the Captain's groin, on the floor, with his gun raised to smash at his head. Mickey got there in two strides, kicked the guy off at the shoulder and hurdled the Captain to follow through. Pain knifed through his head as he struck the wall at an odd angle pinning the other down along the baseboard. The gun waggled toward his face. He used the one he had to club the other's wrist and the gun dropped. There was still some fight left and they rolled over once. Then Mickey found the soft of the other's throat and his thumbs dug deep, pushing. He twisted, heaving, got on his knees. The guy was reaching for Mickey's throat. Mickey released the pressure for a split second. The head flopped forward and he dug again with his thumbs. The guy gasped and rolled away, clutching at his neck. Getting up, Mickey bumped into the Captain, who was reaching for the gun on the floor. There was blood on the Captain's face.

Mickey's breath was sour in his throat. He went to the bedroom, where the other one was rolling from side to side, face down, trying to get up. Mickey helped him with a hand at his belt. The fellow crawled a short distance on his knees, then pushed up to his feet and stumbled into the living room, where the other stood blinking in the harsh light. The Captain had the other one near the door.

They racked the two of them against the wall. The Captain, standing off a little, checked the state of the gun in his hand. He brushed at the blood on his face. He was panting heavily, but his voice came out even and clear and quiet.

"I'm a police officer," he said, "and if you make any more trouble, I can kill you in the line of duty and it will look all right in the book. Now we got some questions, Mickey?"

Mickey wiped his mouth with the back of his hand.

"Where's Teller?" he said. "And Wister?"

They stared at him, blinking. The Captain brushed off some more of the blood and shrugged in his rumpled suit jacket. His eyes were chunks of broken glass between the slits of his eyelids.

"So far," he said, "the only rap against you is impersonating Federal officers and maybe simple assault. Teller and Wister are up for murder. You help us and they'll never touch you."

Mickey picked up the cue.

"You want to walk out there, without the girl," he said, "and explain to Teller how you fouled up? Okay, go ahead."

He pulled the stocky one clear of the door, twisting him to face it. He opened the door wide and reached for the other one. The guy tried to pull back along the wall and the Captain grabbed his coat collar and brought him around fast behind the other. The one in front looked outside and worked his mouth.

"Okay," he said hoarsely. "Shut the goddamn door."

Mickey closed the door with his foot.

"Talk to us," Mickey said.

As in the beginning, the stocky one did the talking.

"We didn't know—only about the girl. They told us to pick up the girl and get her out of the house. That's all."

"Where were you supposed to take her?" the Captain asked. "Just stand around on the grass with her?"

"Just down the street."

"Which way down the street?"

"That way."

He pointed to his left. It would be down toward a section of abandoned stores, and there was a wash down there, Mickey remembered, that you crossed by an old concrete bridge. After that you were heading into the desert.

"How far?" Mickey said.

"I don't know. Just walk her down the street till they met us."

"Where are they now?"

"I don't know, for God's sake!"

Mickey's right fist knotted.

"Where are Teller and Wister?" he said.

The stocky one, watching the fist, tried to back away,

but he was against the wall and had no place to go. He shook his head dumbly.

"Honest to Christ!" the other one said. "We don't know!"

Mickey hit him in the mouth with the back of his hand. The Captain straightened him back up.

"That's true," the stocky one said. "All they told us—get the girl and walk down the street toward the gully."

Mickey looked at the Captain, who nodded. The Captain covered them with the gun while Mickey went to the bedroom and found one of the felt hats. The other one was lying under the overturned armchair where the Captain had made his bid. Mickey pulled it out, shaped it roughly. He put the hats on them, pulling them down tight. He switched off the light, pulled them clear of the door, opened it and gave the stocky one a push.

"All right," he said, "get walking."

"Listen—" the stocky one said.

"More words?" Mickey said.

"No—I don't know no more—"

"Then start thinking. Think while you walk."

He gave the stocky one another push and he stumbled outside. The other one followed. They stood on the flagstones, looking up and down the deserted street. Mickey slammed the door behind them and locked it.

"Stay here," he said to the Captain. "They'll run into Teller and Wister sooner or later."

"Mickey—"

"I'll do it right this time, Captain," he said. "You just

see that nobody gets to Margarita."

"Where is she?"

"In the bathroom."

Mickey went through the kitchen, unlocked the back door and opened it silently. He unhooked the screen door on the service porch, opened that and stepped out onto wet grass. He studied the court carefully and saw nobody. None of the units was lighted.

He looked around the corner of the house toward the front door. The two hired guns were halfway down the walk, standing close together. Mickey guessed that by the kind of deal they probably had with Teller, they had collected half of whatever they would get and, to get the other half, they would have to show up with the girl. Teller would see to it that whatever transportation they had was under his control, so they wouldn't be inclined to run out on him. Therefore, Mickey reasoned, they now had no way to get anywhere except on foot. Teller surely wouldn't let them get far.

Rain dripped from the eaves and ran down his neck. The gun he held was slick with wet and he kept drying his hands alternately on the inside of his coat pockets and shifting the gun from one hand to the other. The stocky one moved forward a couple of paces, but the other held back. The first one gestured vigorously and finally the other went along. They went to the sidewalk, looked down toward the gully, then turned in the opposite direction and walked rapidly toward the more densely settled part of town. It would be a long walk, Mickey thought.

Or maybe, he thought then, a very short one.

They were getting away fast and he sprinted through the wet grass, staying close to the houses along the street, in the deep shadows. He was halfway across the yard of the second house from his own when he heard a car start down the street behind him. The two on the sidewalk heard it at the same time and stopped, then went on, at a dogtrot. Mickey kept step with them, a few paces back. Unexpectedly, the grass left off, there was a stretch of mud and he slipped in it, nearly fell, then caught himself in time and moved more cautiously.

The car seemed a long time coming. There were no headlights yet. He veered closer to the next house he came to and ducked into the shelter of a high shrub growing off the near front corner. A second later the headlights came on and the car swerved, sweeping the walk with light. The two fugitives halted on the walk, turned into a paved driveway and raced to an eight-foot steel-wire gate, nearly invisible in the dark.

It was the end of their trip. The car nosed sharply into the curb. The headlights picked them out against the gate, then went dark. Mickey recognized Teller's car. The two front doors opened simultaneously and Teller got out from under the wheel and walked around the car and up the drive toward the gate, light and quick on his feet for a big man.

Wister got out from the other side. He was wearing the French cap set square on his head and Mickey could see the glint off his thick glasses as he joined Teller on the drive. He dried his left hand in his pocket, put the gun in it, dried his right hand and shifted the gun back again.

There were bushes and a couple of scrubby trees at random in the front yard of the house between him and the four men at the gate. He began to work his way across the wet lawn toward where the big car was nosed in at the drive, both doors still open. The four of them at the gate were talking in low voices. Mickey didn't try to hear what they were saying. It didn't matter very much anymore. By the time he reached the nearer of the open car doors, he couldn't see the two hirelings. They were blocked by Teller's huge frame and Wister's wide, thick one.

He slid into the front seat of the car, found the light switch and slid under the wheel and got one foot on the ground. Then he turned on the lights and moved clear of the car, staying in the shadow of the open door behind the light beam. At the gate, Teller and Wister had twisted and were looking back, shading their eyes against the sudden light. Teller took two steps toward the car.

"Hold it," Mickey said. "I've got a gun and I'll use it."

Teller's heavy face contorted.

"Mr. Marine?" he said.

"My name is Mickey Phillips."

Wister's right hand moved down over his chest.

"Keep it up there," Mickey said. "Now there are four of you. I want you to get in line, Teller first, and walk very slow down this way, till I say stop. You start right now and the first one that gets out of line, I start shooting. I'm a good shot. Now come on!"

There was some shuffling about, but the line didn't form. Mickey squeezed off and under the echo of the report he could hear the whining ricochet over the concrete drive. The four went stiff. Teller started to walk toward him. The two hired hands jumped to follow, but Wister remained to one side, hanging back.

"Come on!" Mickey barked.

Lights went on in the house to his right. A man and woman in night dress appeared in the doorway. They gabbled in excited Spanish.

"Poleecy!" Mickey yelled. "Call the police!"

Wister appeared to slide into line behind Teller. Then suddenly, they had split far apart. Teller was charging straight down the drive toward the car, his frame shaking. Wister had veered off to Mickey's right. The other two ran off toward town, their feet pounding on the wet cement.

Mickey aimed carefully and shot Teller low in the belly. The big man buckled, fell forward, rolled onto the grass. Wister was coming at him across the hood of the car, scrambling. There was a knife in his hand. Mickey, blocked now by the open car door, backed off to get in the clear. Wister slid over the hood, grabbed the door for support and managed to get his balance. He formed a target momentarily, then, as Mickey aimed to shoot, he dived at Mickey's ankles, slashed upward with the knife.

Mickey fell hard in the street. He rolled to keep his head from striking the concrete and felt the knife blade deep in his thigh, a red-hot pain. Wister was clawing his way up over his legs. Mickey twisted desperately, clubbed at the other's head. The blow glanced off to Wister's shoulder and he was still coming. The knife was up in Wister's right hand. Mickey dropped the gun, caught Wister's forearm in both hands and swung it up in a long arc against the normal articulation of the ball-and-socket joint. Wister screamed with pain and rolled away. The knife clattered wetly on the pavement. Mickey reached the car, pulled himself up and stood against the fender, sucking air in huge gasps. Teller crawled around the front of the car on his knees and one hand, holding his belly with the other. Oblivious of Mickey, he groped for the gun Mickey had dropped. Mickey watched him. Nearby he could hear Wister moaning over his broken arm.

Mickey waited till Teller's hand had reached to close on the gun, then he limped over there and kicked the gun away. It slid across the street, banged dully against the opposite curb. Teller's big face looked up at him vaguely.

"You better lie down, Mr. Teller," Mickey said. "You'll bleed to death inside, crawling around like that."

Teller gazed at him for a long moment, then, on his knees, he shook his head to clear it, and found Wister with his eyes. His mouth twisted.

"You stupid son of a bitch," he said, "You dirty white trash scum …"

Mickey turned away and started back toward the house. He felt little pain in his leg now, but it was stiff and he could feel it bleeding badly. He was glad he wouldn't have to walk very far.

The Captain was waiting in the open doorway, the gun dangling from his right hand. Distantly, Mickey could hear a siren. He slipped, entering, and the Captain put out a hand to support him.

"They won't go anywhere," Mickey said. "They're

down there—where the car is. Where's Margarita?"

"Wherever that was you said," the Captain said.

Mickey headed for the bedroom. Behind him, he heard the Captain go outside and start down the flagstone walk. The siren was much closer now.

He found his way through the dark bedroom, knocked lightly on the bathroom door.

"*Sí?*" Margarita said.

"It's me—Joe," Mickey said.

"*Gracias, Madre de Dios,*" he heard her say.

He opened the door and went in. She was sitting, fully dressed, in the bathtub, clutching the edge with both hands, staring at him with her big black eyes. His leg would no longer support him. He went down on his knees beside the tub and reached for her. When the Captain found them sometime later, he had his head on Margarita's shoulder and they were whispering to each other, things about "*Meh-hico,*" and "*pueblo,*" and Margarita was brushing the mud out of his hair and off the back of his torn, wet jacket, so he would be clean when the time came to start home; the long way home …

THE END

THOMAS B. DEWEY BIBLIOGRAPHY
(1915-1981)

Novels

Mac series:
Draw the Curtain Close (1947; reprinted as *Dame in Danger*, 1958)
Every Bet's a Sure Thing (1953)
Prey for Me (1954; UK as *The Case of the Murdered Model*, 1955)
The Mean Streets (1955)
The Brave, Bad Girls (1956)
You've Got Him Cold (1958)
The Case of the Chased and the Unchaste (1959)
The Girl Who Wasn't There (1960; reprinted as *The Girl Who Never Was*, 1962)
How Hard to Kill (1962)
A Sad Song Singing (1963)
Don't Cry for Long (1964)
Portrait of a Dead Heiress (1965)
Deadline (1967)
Death and Taxes (1967)
The King Killers (1968; UK as *Death Turns Right*, 1969)
The Love-Death Thing (1969)
The Taurus Trip (1970)

Pete Schoefield series:
And Where She Stops (1957; UK as *I.O.U. Murder*, 1958)
Go to Sleep, Jeannie (1959)
Too Hot for Hawaii (1960)
The Golden Hooligan (1961; UK as *Mexican Slayride*, 1961)
Go, Honeylou (1962)
The Girl with the Sweet Plump Knees (1963)

The Girl in the Punchbowl (1964)
Only on Tuesdays (1964)
Nude in Nevada (1965)

Singer Batts series:
Hue and Cry (1944; reprinted as *Room for Murder*, 1950;
    UK as *The Murder of Marion Mason*, 1951)
As Good as Dead (1946)
Mourning After (1950)
Handle With Fear (1951)

Unrelated Mysteries:
My Love is Violent (1956)
Hunter at Large (1961)
Can a Mermaid Kill (1965)
A Season for Violence (1966)

As Tom Brandt:
Kiss Me Hard (1954)
Run, Brother, Run! (1954)

As Cord Wainer:
Mountain Girl (1953)

Short Stories

"You've Got Him Cold" (1965, Simon & Schuster)
"Never Send to Know" (January 1965, *Ellery Queen's
    Mystery Magazine*)
"The Prevalence of Monsters" (April 1965, *Ellery Queen's
    Mystery Magazine*)
"The Big Job" (December 1965, *The Saint Mystery
    Magazine*; Mac)
"Lucien's Nose" (July 1966, *Ellery Queen's Mystery
    Magazine*)

Thomas Blanchard Dewey was born on March 6, 1915 in Elkhart, Indiana. He graduated from Kansas State Teachers College and then became an editor at Storycraft, Inc., a Hollywood correspondence school. He went to work as an  administrative assistant for the State Department in Washington DC in the mid-1940s before joining an advertising firm in Los Angeles. Dewey began his writing career with *Hue and Cry* in 1944 featuring amateur sleuth Singer Batts. He went on to create two more series characters, Pete Schofield and Mac, one of the most believable and humane PIs in crime fiction. Dewey made a living as a full time novelist from 1952-1971, until he stopped writing and became an assistant professor of English at Arizona State University until 1977. He died in April of 1981 in Tempe, Arizona.

Made in the USA
Columbia, SC
16 September 2024

41725559R00135